TROUBLE AT NATHAN'S FORD

When a night bank robbery in Drystone City goes horribly wrong, Cage turns his back on lawlessness and heads home. But when he arrives in the border town of Nathan's Ford, he rides into tragedy: his father's ranch has been burned to the ground, killing his parents, and his brother is on the run. And there's even worse news: the Drystone bank owner has ridden into town, armed to the teeth — seeking to avenge the death of his wife at the hands of the robbers . . .

Books by Jack Sheriff
in the Linford Western Library:

BURY HIM DEEP, IN TOMBSTONE
THE MAN FROM THE
STAKED PLAINS
INCIDENT AT POWDER RIVER
BLACK DAY AT HANGDOG
KID KANTRELL
STARLIGHT
BILLY SUNDOWN
THE KILLING AT CIRCLE C
THE LAST WATER-HOLE
THE CHICANERY OF PACO IBANEZ
THE HUNTING OF LOPE GAMBOA
OUTLAW CANYON

JACK SHERIFF

TROUBLE AT NATHAN'S FORD

Complete and Unabridged

LINFORD
Leicester

First published in Great Britain in 2013 by
Robert Hale Limited
London

First Linford Edition
published 2016
by arrangement with
Robert Hale Limited
London

A catalogue record for this book is available from the British Library.

ISBN 978–1–4448–2899–3

Published by
F. A. Thorpe (Publishing)
Anstey, Leicestershire

Set by Words & Graphics Ltd.
Anstey, Leicestershire
Printed and bound in Great Britain by
T. J. International Ltd., Padstow, Cornwall

This book is printed on acid-free paper

1

They broke camp soon after midnight, the 'breed, Ramos, kicking damp earth over the fire's dying embers, Cage prowling restlessly, gazing through the trees and off to the west, his mind and his nerves grappling with what lay ahead. Last chance, or a new beginning? Who could say? But if things went badly wrong, this time there would be no long prison sentence. Instead there would be the raw smell of fresh-sawn timber, the sound of six-inch nails being hammered into wood to construct the gallows from which long hemp ropes would be hung to stretch both their necks.

He saw Ramos watching him, dark eyes glinting, teeth white against his swarthy skin as he grinned and, with a surge of anger, Cage sent his cigarette hissing into the damp grass and walked to the horses. A soft whicker greeted him. Metal jingled as the roan turned its head, and leather creaked as Cage swung into the saddle.

They rode out from under the trees and down to the river in pale moonlight softened by a thin mist floating like smoke across the flat water, then turned their horses to the west and rode without haste along the grassy bank. They were, Cage reckoned, five miles from the one main street of Drystone City, a sprawl of dwellings and business premises on the Texas plains. More to the point, they were a mile closer to the white mansion built by Milton Guthrie, the owner of the Drystone Citizens' Bank.

Four miles to Guthrie's place. A half-hour's easy ride.

'You want I threaten him with the knife?' Ramos said. 'Or what? Put fear into his wife, maybe?' Again the flash of white teeth as he grinned. 'She is young, old — or what? You think if I tell him I rape his wife he will give them to us, *los llaves*, the keys?'

'We want him, *and* his keys,' Cage said. 'The keys open the doors. The safe will have a combination lock. To open that we need Guthrie.'

'Nevertheless,' Ramos said happily, 'we must threaten. I anticipate with relish. If he has red blood in his veins, he will fight, there will be violence.'

'Forget it. A man startled out of his sleep in the early hours, dragged out of bed in his nightshirt,' Cage said, 'is a pale shadow.'

'You think?'

'I spent two years thinking, in a hot, roach-infested cell in a Texas penitentiary. Realized that what put me there was another man's folly, my own stupidity: I went along with him when he said there were easy pickings to be had from robbing banks in broad daylight.'

'It has been done, many times.'

'And men have died.'

'So now . . . ?'

'Dead of night. Street deserted. We

open the door with keys, walk in the bank like we own the place. The safe's opened for us. We walk out, very rich.'

'You think?'

Cage flashed him a look.

'I know.'

They rode the rest of the way in silence. From time to time Ramos slid the big knife he carried out of its worn leather sheath. The blade glinted in the moonlight. Once he held the knife by clamping the blade between his white teeth, glanced across at Cage. Took it out, with one flick sent it spinning into the air to catch it deftly by the hilt.

Cage shook his head in disbelief. For the first of his years inside he'd had a skinny lizard for company, staring unblinkingly from the hot stone wall. Ramos had been his cell mate for most of the second year. The 'breed, Cage estimated, was in his late twenties — a few years younger than Cage — and his actions at the best of times suggested he was halfway to loco. Cage had to admit that if Guthrie proved stubborn, a man with the menace that Ramos exuded, like a skunk exuded stink, could tip the scales their way.

They came upon the mansion suddenly, riding away from where the river looped, then around a stand of dusty cottonwoods that had been hiding the big house from view. That brought them close to the trail into Drystone City. Guthrie had erected his mansion there, set back fifty feet. The banker had planted trees along one side of the house as a windbreak. The white house stood out in stark contrast to the dark trees. No lights showed in its windows. The night was warm. There was no movement in the air, no breath of wind.

'Maybe he has dogs,' Ramos said.

'Soon find out,' Cage said.

He rode across the trail to the trees. Swung down. Loose-tied the roan to a low branch. Ramos left his horse to graze on the grass, ground-tethered. He strutted towards the picket fence, slim in his flared Mex' pants, his shirt with its loose sleeves. The knife in its sheath was at his left hip, the hilt jutting. The holster carrying an ancient six-gun was strapped to his right thigh with a rawhide thong.

He tipped back his fringed black and gold sombrero, glanced at Cage.

'No dogs yapping, waking the dead. But there are stables behind the house. Perhaps they are there, sleeping. You think?'

'Ramos, will you for Christ's sake quit asking me what I think?'

The 'breed grinned. 'What I think is, you are the man with knowledge. I value your opinion. For example, this way of acquiring wealth is *muy ingenioso*, it — '

Cage opened the gate and started up the path. In the stillness his boots crunched. He stepped on to the grass, moved silently through the glistening dew. He eyed the windows, the solid oak front door. Guthrie would have the keys to the bank. But first they had to get into the house without — what had Ramos said, waking the dead? But

Guthrie wasn't dead, just sleeping. Though, before the night was over . . .

Ramos went past him with a whisper of sound. The 'breed pivoted, a matador playing the bull, stepped gracefully up to the front door and tried the handle. The door swung open on oiled hinges.

'The bedrooms,' Ramos said softly. 'Upstairs, and at the front of the house — you think?'

Cage grunted. He stepped into a hallway, clicked the door shut. For a moment he leant back against the warm panels. He could feel his Colt hanging heavy against his thigh. It was a comforting presence, but one he had no intention of using. Unless . . . unless . . .

The stairs were directly ahead, wide, carpeted. Ramos was already halfway up, light on his feet, a dark ghost in the gloom. Then there was movement at his hip, a faint swish and the flash of steel. Cage knew the 'breed had drawn his knife.

'No,' he said softly.

He caught up with the man, grasped his arm, held him still.

Listened.

To a man snoring.

Ramos lifted a hand and pointed left, turned his head. The sombrero's fringes danced, the looped neck cord swung one way, then back, and again Cage thought of hemp, of rope. He released the 'breed's arm, nodded, yes, that way. They crept along the landing, flat against the wall. The snoring was coming from behind the first door. It was ajar. Ramos shrugged, pushed it open and slipped inside.

Behind him, Cage saw the big four-poster bed, the white frilled drapes held back by cords, the man and woman lying asleep beneath rumpled covers, a brightly coloured patchwork quilt. The man was closest to them. He was lying on his back, his mouth open.

Cage pointed to the woman. Her hair was dark, spread across the plump pillow. Ramos grinned, went around the bed.

The snoring broke off with a strangled sound as Cage slapped a hand on the man's shoulder. His eyes started open. He blinked, then came fully awake with a jerk and his head shot around as he stared at Cage.

'Time to get up, Guthrie,' Cage said. 'A couple of your valued customers want to make a large withdrawal.'

The banker tried to clear his throat, choked, struggled to rise.

'What the . . . what the . . . ?'

Cage tightened his grip, took hold of a handful of hair and jerked the man out from under the covers. He hit the floor on his naked backside. His teeth clicked. He moaned softly.

Cage used both hands to yank him to his feet by the front of his nightshirt, slammed him back against one of the bed's uprights.

'When I let go, put your pants on. Tuck the shirt in. Put on a pair of boots. Then get the keys to the bank.'

'That's not possible.'

Cage hit him. His fist travelled six inches. He split the banker's lip. Guthrie's head cracked against the timber. From the other side of the bed there came a soft sound, swiftly stifled. When Cage glanced across, the woman was staring at her husband. Ramos had his hand clamped across her mouth. The big knife's blade was pressed to the soft flesh of her throat.

'The keys are held by the town marshal,' Guthrie croaked wetly. Blood was trickling down his chin, staining the white shirt. 'You see, we find that's the safest — '

'I don't believe you.'

'But it's true, we always anticipated — '

'I don't believe you, but I might believe your wife.'

'My wife?'

'My friend with the knife is going to ask her if you are telling the truth.'

'No.' Despite the knife held against her throat, Guthrie's wife shook her head violently. That one word, muffled by Ramos's hand, was clear in its meaning.

'Let her speak,' Cage said.

Ramos removed his hand. His dark eyes shone in the gloom. The knife's blade remained at the woman's throat, the razor-sharp edge drawing a tiny bead of blood.

She said, 'Milt, don't be a fool, give them the keys.'

'You know I can't do that.'

'Then I'm going to die, but of course you'd like that, wouldn't you?'

Guthrie actually sneered. 'Surely it's the other way round — '

'I don't know what we've walked into here,' Cage said to the woman, 'but that's not what we'd like. We want those keys, but on their own they're not enough. He has to ride with us into town.'

'Then that's what he'll do,' she said, and suddenly there was something different in the woman's voice; a scathing, waspish tone to it when she spoke to her husband. 'You hear me, Milt Guthrie. You do as you're damn well told. Put on your pants, if you can find them and they still fit, then go downstairs and get those keys.'

Across the four-poster bed, the banker's eyes met those of his wife. A silent message passed between them. What Cage saw was a burning hatred. It seemed mutual. At the same time, Milt Guthrie visibly relaxed, and slowly nodded his head as if a decision had been reached.

'Yes,' Guthrie said. 'All right, I'll do that. At least, that way . . . '

He was a big man, dark-haired, perhaps in his forties. Cage stood back and watched for the few moments it took Guthrie to dress. Then, clearly understanding that the keys were but a part of it and for the rest they needed him alive, Guthrie led the way out of the room and down the stairs.

'Wait here,' he said, heading for the rear of the house.

'If you come back with a gun,' Cage

said, 'your wife will be the first to die.'

The threat was treated with an amused stare. Then the banker was gone. Within seconds he was back, a big bunch of keys jingling in his hand. He brushed past Cage, grabbed his hat from a peg and strode out of the house.

'I'll saddle up,' he said, and was gone, making for the stables.

There was no sign of the 'breed.

'Ramos,' Cage called, 'we're done here, let's move out.'

Without waiting for a reply he walked easily down the path. He was in the saddle and waiting when Guthrie rode around the side of the house on a fine palomino. He joined Cage. Both of them looked back at the house.

'Where is he, your . . . friend?'

Guthrie said nothing.

The front door was wide open. There was no movement in the shadowy interior.

Guthrie said softly, 'It would be in my wife's character to say something to him, something that might enrage — '

And then whatever he was about to say was cut short as Ramos came jogging out of the house holding aloft a bottle of amber liquid.

'He found your liquor store,' Cage said, almost sagging in the saddle so intense was his relief.

'Then let's get this over with,' Milton Guthrie said, and he spat blood into the dust before turning the big palomino and spurring away from them.

2

Drystone City consisted of one wide main street that curved to the right as it followed the land's gently undulating contours. The tall false-fronted buildings — unlit, coated in the dust of ages — gave the impression that the three men were riding into an isolated, deserted ghost town. That feeling was dispelled as they drew nearer, rode in. Several lanterns hung from rusting iron brackets, casting a glow over the warped boards of the plankwalks. Some way ahead of them, where the street curved, a light shone in the window of a single-storey building built from local sandstone.

'Someone's up late,' Cage said. And he cast a glance to his left and drew rein.

'Or early,' Ramos said. The half-empty bottle clinked against his teeth.

'Dave Eyke's marriage is on the rocks,' Guthrie said, folding his hands on the saddle horn.

Cage squinted down the street. 'That where he lives?'

'Where he works.'

'So if that's his office, where does he sleep?'

'If he manages any sleep at all,' Guthrie said, 'it'll be in one of the empty cells.' He caught Cage's swift look, and said, 'Dave Eyke's the town marshal. That's the jail you're looking at.'

'Jail is of no importance,' Ramos said grandly. 'Your bank, however, is *muy importante* and, as such, I estimate it will be a tall building, a very fine establishment.' He looked at Cage, and grinned. 'You think?'

'I think it'll be the building over there, the one bearing the name Drystone Citizen's Bank,' Cage said, dismounting.

Guthrie slid from the saddle.

'You need these,' he said, and he

tossed the bunch of keys to Cage.

'We need you,' Cage said, 'to open the safe.'

'I intend to do as little as possible to help. You are about to rob me and the ranchers and other businessmen who entrust me with their money. You want to go in, open the doors yourself.'

Why not? Cage thought. He'd spent most of his adult life drifting, the last two years in jail. Yet here he was, standing in front of a bank, the keys in his hand.

He shook his head in disbelief, walked past the hitch rail to the big building with its double doors, high, secured windows. Looks like a jail itself, he thought, and was vaguely aware of the sound of the horses as the two men followed him.

Then he was at the door, jingling the keys, looking for the right one.

But, right away, he could see that there was no right one. No key on the ring was even close to being large enough to fit into the big keyhole without rattling around like a dry stone in a tin can.

He swung around.

Guthrie was standing by the hitch rail. Ramos was still on his horse, the empty whiskey bottle dangling from his hand.

'They're my house keys,' Guthrie said. 'I told you, but you wouldn't believe me: I leave the bank's keys with Dave Eyke, he locks them in his safe.'

'And, if it is of any importance,' Ramos said, tossing the bottle in the general direction of the alley separating the bank from the next block, 'there is a man now walking up the street from the jail. He has seen Guthrie. No doubt he will be bringing the keys to allow the man to enter his place of business. You think?'

'At three in the morning?' Cage said. 'Think again, Ramos.'

'If it is trouble, that is no problem. I am friendly with trouble, trouble is my constant companion — '

'You got a problem up there, Milt?'

Cage couldn't hold back a broad grin.

'You should ask my friend, not Guthrie,' he called to the approaching lawman. 'He has a wonderful way with words.'

'I'll ask you instead: what the hell's going on?'

Marshal Dave Eyke was tall and grey-haired, his eyes a cold blue, the badge a glittering shield on his vest. He had not drawn his gun, but his hand was casually brushing the butt.

'Guthrie was concerned about his bank's security,' Cage said. 'We rode into town with him to allay his fears.'

'Sounds like you're as mouthy as your friend, and a poor liar to boot.' Eyke looked keenly at the banker, at his split lip, the dried blood on his chin. 'You walk into a door, Milt?'

'A fist swung by this feller.' Guthrie nodded at Cage. 'Leaving my keys in your safe has at last been justified. These two broke into my house, threatened me and my wife, forced me to ride into town. They wanted my keys so they could get into the bank. Once inside, they were going to force me to open the safe.'

The marshal nodded. With a slick, practised movement, he drew his six-gun and made a big show of cocking the hammer.

'So this is where I say you're both under arrest for attempting to rob the Drystone Citizens' Bank,' Eyke said. He looked at Ramos, gestured with the gun. 'You, get down off that horse. Then both of you walk ahead of me down the street, hands up around your shoulders. If you think I'm too old to shoot good, then you're welcome to make a run for it.'

'And just to make sure we do exactly as he says,' Cage said to Guthrie, 'you might as well bring out that gun you've got tucked down the back of your pants.'

Their movements since they had entered town had left Cage and Ramos positioned at a disadvantage. Cage had walked a short way down a gradual slope to the bank when he tried the keys. Ramos's mount had walked unchecked in the same direction, the 'breed fully occupied with the stolen whiskey. Guthrie had walked with his horse to the hitch rail, and that was where he'd stayed. So now Marshal Dave Eyke was in front of them, in the middle of the street, Guthrie behind them at the hitch rail.

Even as those thoughts flashed through Cage's mind, he heard the click of another gun cocking and knew he'd been right: back at the house, when Guthrie went for his keys, he had picked up a pistol.

And so without conscious thought — perhaps again visualizing the hangman's rope — Cage swivelled, flung the heavy bunch of keys at the marshal's face and made a run for the alley.

How much had Ramos drunk? A whole bottle? Could he still function? Would he use the six-gun, or his favoured knife?

The answer came as Cage dived, hit the ground rolling and came to his feet in deep shadow amid broken wooden boxes and rattling tin cans. A mangy cat hissed and darted away. Then the night air was split by the crack of a six-gun, followed by a roar of pain from Milt Guthrie. A second shot barked, then a third.

Drawing his Colt, Cage poked his head out of the alley.

Under fire from Eyke, Ramos had turned his horse and spurred away. Then, feeling the wind of the marshal's bullets, he'd slid from the saddle and was using the animal as a living shield. The most that could be seen of him was the big sombrero, the shine of his dark eyes. He was resting his right wrist on the saddle, firing spaced shots at the marshal. Dave Eyke had sprinted for the plankwalk across the street from the bank, and was half hidden in a doorway. At the hitch rail Milt Guthrie was down behind his horse, rocking on his knees and clutching his left shoulder.

Cage was out of it and clear, if he so chose. He could run, he knew that. The alley would lead to the edge of town. He had no horse — but so what? He'd been afoot more than once in his life.

But there was the question of Ramos, and what allegiance Cage owed the 'breed he had shared a cell with for twelve long months. For now Ramos was holding his own, perhaps doing a little better than that. But Eyke was a lawman, facing a bank robber, and of an age and experience in which sentiment would play no part. And he wanted his man.

Even as the thought crossed Cage's mind, there was a bright muzzle flash. Eyke had stepped out and fired a carefully aimed shot. Ramos's horse snorted, lifted its head, its eyes rolling white. Then it sagged, its knees buckled, and it went down kicking. Ramos went with it. Desperate for cover as Eyke began pumping shots across the street, he flattened himself behind his dying mount.

Cage took a deep breath, let it go in frustration. Then he poked his gun around the edge of the building and fired three fast shots. They punched into timber alongside Eyke. He backed off, tripped and fell headlong into the doorway. At once Ramos came to his feet. He blasted a shot at Guthrie that kicked dirt into the wounded banker's face as he struggled futilely to rise, then swung to bring fire to bear on the marshal.

'No,' Cage yelled. 'Get away now. Use Guthrie's horse. Lead mine, I'll meet you outside town.'

A bullet from the irate marshal chipped splinters from the building by Cage as he carelessly swung his arm in a high circle, telling Ramos where he wanted him.

Ramos's teeth flashed in a grin. The sombrero had slipped from his head and was held across his shoulders by its plaited cord. His dark, greased hair shone in the moonlight. The big knife flapped heavily at his hip as he moved away from his dead horse. Guthrie's palamino was at the hitch rail, reins trailing, shivering. Ramos went for it at a lazy jog. That put his back to the marshal — and the meaning in the words Cage yelled had not been lost on Eyke.

'Stop right there,' Eyke called, 'or so help me I'll put a bullet in your back.'

And again Cage drove him into the shelter of the doorway with a shot that clipped the marshal's Stetson. He sent another that kept Eyke back in the shadows; looked across at Ramos, saw him swing agilely into Guthrie's saddle then wheel the horse and lean down like an Indian to scoop up the trailing reins of Cage's roan.

Then the 'breed was gone. He flattened himself in the saddle and spurred Guthrie's palamino furiously up the wide street, Cage's roan behind him, stirrups flapping.

Ignoring Cage, Eyke stepped out of the doorway and blasted a shot after the two racing horses. But Ramos was already out of effective six-gun range. Dust spurted, showing how far short the marshal's bullet had fallen. And when, with his next attempt, his hammer clicked on a spent cartridge, Eyke rammed the gun furiously into its holster and stood, hands on hips, staring at the receding cloud of dust.

Cage stepped back into the alley, and began to pick his way through the rubbish that was now all that lay between him and safety.

* * *

Ramos had correctly interpreted Cage's signal from the alley, and once clear of town had circled around to the east. The 'breed had found an old cattle trail, tethered both horses in a stand of dry, stunted trees, then stood out in the open. He was smoking a cigarette when Cage came up to him half an hour later.

'It was easy, the getaway,' Ramos said. 'But we came away without seeing the inside of the bank. That is unfortunate. By this time, I was expecting to be a rich man . . . ' He shrugged eloquently.

'If they decide to raise a posse and give chase, you'll be poor, and dead.'

'But why would they waste all that energy? We are failed bank robbers. We escaped with much flair. It might be considered that the marshal has lost face — but there was only Guthrie to witness his shame, so it is of no consequence. And Guthrie? He has a flesh wound. His bank is intact.' Again Ramos shrugged, and his smile was sly. 'There are, of course,' he said, 'many other banks . . . '

'Not for me,' Cage said, and he turned towards the waiting roan. 'I've been away from home for far too long. I'm going to put that right before it's too damn late.'

3

The ride across Texas took Cage the best part of a week. He had expected to make the trip on his own, but when he told Ramos he was heading for the river that formed the border between Texas and Mexico, the 'breed rode with him. On that first moonlit night, Cage had made it clear that at some stage they must part company, but at the end of those seven days it was not one but two dusty, trail-worn drifters who rode into Nathan's Ford. The crossing was a sprawling township on the eastern bank of the Rio Grande. The breeze coming off the mighty river touched sun-dried skin like a soothing balm. The scent of its cool waters brought tired horses back to life, put a spring in their step.

Cage and Ramos rode down Main Street, stunned into silence by the afternoon crowds, the horses and wagons, after the emptiness of the vast plains. Cage stayed with the 'breed as far as the Wayfarer Saloon. There, he drew rein. There was no need for talk. During seven days on the trail there had been enough of that, and there was little left to be said.

'We part here,' he said. 'I thank you for your company, Ramos, and no doubt I'll see you about town from time to time.'

He reached across, slapped the surprised 'breed on the shoulder, then turned and rode back the way they had come. But only so far. On the way into town his eyes had been drinking in the familiar sights. He had been away from his home town for fifteen years, leaving Nathan's Ford as a restless young man of eighteen. But from his observations he could see that little had changed. In particular, the same brass plate with its engraved *Attorney at Law* hung outside the same nondescript office that lay somewhat forlornly between the twin bulks of Elliott's livery barn and the town's only hotel, the Alhambra.

There was a hitch rack outside the office. Cage dismounted, tied his horse. He tapped lightly on the door, heard a faint response, gripped the brass door handle and walked in.

The slightly built man behind the desk wore a white shirt, a dark suit. His hair was white and thinning, combed over a mottled scalp. He was bent over papers spreading from an open manila file, a gold pen in one hand. He glanced up, peering over the top of half-frame spectacles that rested almost at the tip of his nose. He smiled.

'Yes sir, what can I do for you?'

Cage cleared his throat.

'I think what I'd like most of all,' he said, 'is for you to shake hands with a ghost from the past.'

* * *

'I cannot believe it,' John Lawrence said. 'That you should arrive now is

. . . well, I've said it, of course: it's unbelievable.'

'Am I getting a sense of foreboding here?' Cage said. 'There's an old saying, warns about stepping out of the frying pan into something very much hotter. Is that what I've done?'

The handshakes were over. Lawrence had wrung Cage's hand as if trying to rip it off, and there had been such a flurry of emotions crossing the old lawyer's face that even then Cage had felt a tremor of unease. He had watched Lawrence rise from his desk, take two glasses and a decanter from a cabinet and pour generous measures of whiskey. They had clinked glasses, and each had taken a sip of what Cage knew was the most expensive whiskey he had ever tasted. It was then that Lawrence had shaken his head, sat down heavily and expressed his disbelief.

'It all depends,' he said, in answer to Cage's question. 'Your relationship with Al and May Butler was . . . well, you know what I'm going to say. You were adopted, so those two lovely people were not blood relatives — '

'Were not? Shouldn't that be are not?'

Lawrence nodded, sadness in his grey eyes. 'I'm extremely sorry, Cage. You are on your way home, I know, after a very long absence. But I'm afraid you are too late to see them. Al and May died one week ago today.'

'Both of them?' Cage said, and now, not surprisingly, along with shock he could hear his own voice expressing utter disbelief.

Again Lawrence nodded.

'Then there's something wrong,' Cage said bluntly. 'Two people do not die on the same day of natural causes. So, what was it, an accident? A cattle stampede, wagon overturning?'

'They died in a terrible fire at the family home. It happened in the dead of night, so in that respect we must thank God they were sleeping.' He shrugged helplessly. 'They were almost certainly suffocated by smoke before being . . . taken by the flames. Death would have been painless.' He paused, giving the terrible thoughts time to fade. 'The fire started on the gallery — old, dry timber, it went up like kindling and the property was totally destroyed.'

'That doesn't answer my question, John.'

Lawrence shook his head. 'No. It was not an accident. The fire was started deliberately.'

'And where was Matt when this was going on?'

'Your brother . . . ' Lawrence hesitated. To Cage, he seemed to be wondering how to proceed, as if he were now treading on dangerous ground. The lawyer looked broodingly into his glass, then up at Cage.

'For the past few years now, Mexican bandits have been active. Your father's spread is close to the river, and the river is the border between Mexico and the USA. Because Al ran one of the smaller outfits, that made him vulnerable. He lost a lot of cattle to those Mexican rustlers, and was unable to replace them because without cattle he could not earn any money. He was unable to raise the capital he needed to survive, and was about to lose everything.'

'I've been away a long time,' Cage said thoughtfully, 'but I always made sure my family could reach me. Matt pleaded with me more than once to send as much cash as I could afford. He didn't once tell me why it was needed.'

'When was the last time that happened?'

Cage shrugged. 'A couple of weeks ago.'

'And did you . . . did you have any money you could send; that you did send?'

Cage smiled, thinking of Drystone City, the 'breed Ramos and the bank robbery that had failed in a blaze of gunfire.

'No,' he said. 'No, I never did have any loose change I could spare.'

'Then in answer to your question I

can tell you that when fire broke out at your parents' spread, Matt was living in a remote line cabin.'

Cage frowned. 'I don't understand. If there were no cattle — '

'Twenty-four hours before Al and May died, Matt made a desperate attempt to come up with the money they needed.' The lawyer looked keenly at Cage.

Instinctively, Cage knew where Lawrence was heading. He pursed his lips. 'What are people saying — that he robbed a bank?'

'Yes,' Lawrence said. 'And it's much more than a malicious rumour. Matt was on the run from the law.'

Cage was still staring at John Lawrence, dumbfounded, when the street door clicked open. A big man stepped into the office, doffing his Stetson. There was a badge pinned to his vest, a worn six-gun at his hip. He glanced at Cage, then grinned across at Lawrence.

'Too busy today, John?'

'By no means,' Lawrence said. 'Cage, I'd like you to renew your acquaintance with Frank Bellard, who's been our town marshal for more years than he cares to remember. Frank pops in every afternoon at around this time and we chew the fat over a drink or two.'

'Cage?' Bellard said, a question in his deep voice as he held out his hand. 'The young man who always insisted he had just the one name?' He grinned. 'Don't I recall you leaving town when you were, what, eighteen years old? Seems I've heard bits and pieces of news about you drifting back from time to time, all of it good. But, hell, you're Al and May Butler's adopted son, so this is surely a tragic homecoming.'

'In more ways than one,' Cage said, taking the proffered hand. 'My parents dead, and I've been told my brother's in a heap of trouble.'

'Until we discover where your brother's holed up, we're unlikely to know the true story,' Bellard said, and Cage flicked a look at Lawrence, caught the almost imperceptible shake of the lawyer's head.

'And as if I haven't got enough on my plate,' Bellard went on, 'a man's hit town with a haunted look on his face and enough weaponry hooked on belt and saddle to equip an army.'

Lawrence shook his head wearily. 'Not another outlaw making a run for the border?'

'Nope, just the opposite,' Bellard said. He rounded the desk, helped himself to a glass and poured a generous slug of the fine, smooth whiskey. 'This fellow is a banker, he tells me, and he's here on a mission.'

Cage went cold.

'Seems a couple of hardcases tried to rob his bank over in Drystone City,' Bellard said, leaning back against the cabinet as he savoured the whiskey. 'Failed, as it happens, but their idea had been to call at the banker's house, use his keys to get at the money.'

Lawrence raised an eyebrow. 'Is this

something we could see more of in the future?'

'I don't know about that,' Bellard said, 'but in this case they threatened the banker. Used some violence, not severe, but enough to break his resistance. Then, when they left the house, one of them, a mean-looking 'breed, lingered in the house. The banker was married, as you'd expect. This feller, half white, half Mex, cut his wife's throat from ear to ear. Left her lying across the breakfast table, her white shirt blood-soaked, her face in a pool of her own blood.'

4

Marshal Frank Bellard said that he had advised the vengeful banker to first slake his thirst at the Wayfarer saloon, then wander down to the jail later that afternoon to give a full account of what had happened in Drystone City, and his reasons for riding to Nathan's Ford.

On the face of it, that was the sensible and lawful way to proceed, but Cage was a step ahead of Bellard. Cage had left Ramos outside the Wayfarer. If Ramos and Guthrie now came face to face, the confrontation would be violent. In a fight with fists, knives or six-guns, small-town banker Guthrie would be the underdog. The outcome was inevitable: Guthrie would die.

With the terrible fear burning within him that he might already be too late to come between the two men, Cage left John Lawrence's office with a calm exterior masking his awful forebodings — the two men accepting with thanks his reasonable excuse of not wanting to disturb their afternoon get-together.

Half-a-dozen horses were dozing at the hitch rail outside the saloon when Cage arrived there on his roan. He quickly dismounted and tied his horse, noting that amongst the ragged ponies there were several horses of quality. One of those would be Guthrie's. Of the others, Cage recognized the palamino Ramos had stolen from the banker.

Inside the Wayfarer the single big room reeked of alcohol, its atmosphere blue with the smoke from cigarettes and cheroots. Cage stepped to one side of the door, the better to see without being noticed. Not that it mattered a damn. The men lining the bar all had a booted foot hooked on the brass rail and were clutching glasses; Cage was staring at a long line of broad backs. The poker players at the tables were also oblivious of his presence, frowning at the cards they'd been dealt or trying not to smirk triumphantly when they realized they held a winning hand. Others not playing but sitting drinking and smoking were slumped back in their chairs and staring with undisguised lust at a slender woman with a tumble of dark wavy hair. Wearing a yellow dress as pale as winter moonlight, she was behind the bar with both hands thrust into the front pocket of her scarlet apron.

Alongside her, casually conversing, was a big man in a dark suit. His shirt was a splash of white in the general gloom, a black string tie with silver tips an affectation that looked in keeping with his bearing of quiet arrogance. His swept-back hair was snow white. A gold watch chain looped across his vest emphasized the generous swell of his midriff.

The men playing poker were Mexicans. One of them, his back to Cage, had a big fringed red and gold sombrero across his shoulders, greasy hair as black as a raven's wing.

It was Ramos.

At the bar, one man out of the dozen standing there had finished his drink and turned to face the room. His eyes were busy, studying one table then moving on to the next, squinting through the hanging smoke. He was a big man. His lower lip was swollen. He was clearly favouring his left shoulder. The heavy Colt revolver at his right hip was worn high, not tied to his thigh in the fashion of a gunfighter — but this was no gunfighter. This was the Drystone City banker, Milton Guthrie.

Even as Cage spotted him, cursed under his breath and moved away from the door, the banker's searching gaze picked out Ramos. His face darkened. Without hesitation he stepped clear of the bar and fumbled awkwardly for his six-gun.

Still clawing at the butt, he started towards Ramos.

Cage moved to cut him off.

Swiftly, he threaded his way between

the tables. In his haste he kicked a table leg. The flimsy contraption rocked, tilted. A full glass tipped, rolled, splashing beer over a bearded man's pants before falling to shatter on the hard, sawdust-covered floor. That drew an angry, spluttering protest from the man with the whiskers, quelled by a menacing look from Cage. But the accident that broke a glass also broke Guthrie's concentration. The stare that had been fixed on Ramos flashed across to Cage — and again there was instant recognition.

The sound of glass splintering had also drawn the young woman's gaze. Her green eyes picked out Guthrie and Cage, saw the deadly purpose in their eyes, the tension in their demeanour. It dawned on her that both men were making for one particular table. Touching the sleeve of the big man who stood beside her, she looked for the reason.

The Mexicans, no strangers to violence, had also spotted Guthrie and

Cage. Worn pasteboards drifted like autumn leaves as several of them threw down their cards and scrambled away from the tables. Ramos remained. He had turned without concern to watch Milton Guthrie's approach, and the watching woman instantly drew the right conclusions.

Without once looking away from the trouble she knew was about to explode she called sharply to a burly barman chatting further down the line of drinkers. Already alerted by the change in the atmosphere, he snapped a glance at the room then dipped beneath the bar and came up with a heavy wooden stave. Made sluggish by the alcohol they'd consumed and a reluctance to be disturbed, the drinkers at the bar were beginning to turn, still clutching shot glasses or beer mugs.

The woman watched them with a disbelieving shake of the head. Then, as if it was something she did every day at around this same time, she casually pulled a tiny, shining derringer pistol from under her apron, and folded her arms.

All this had happened in mere fractions of seconds. And it had taken that length of time and more for Guthrie to get his fingers firmly around the butt of his six-gun and draw it from the awkwardly placed holster, still more precious time for his thumb to clumsily pull back the hammer.

Two of the Mexicans with Ramos had glanced at him, seen a message in his eyes, and continued playing. Then, when Guthrie had almost reached the 'breed, both of them flung down their playing cards and sent chairs flying in a scatter of splintered wood as they stood to confront the banker.

One was a mean-looking character with a patch over one eye and long hair restrained by a dirty red headband, more Apache than Mexican. Another was as skinny as a starving rabbit, and was toting a rusty Dragoon Colt.

Ramos, sombrero flapping like a coloured cape, sprang from the table.

He moved with the agility of a cat. There was a swish of smooth leather as he ripped the knife from its sheath. In the dim light the blade flashed wickedly.

Cage was still several tables away from Guthrie. Ramos was much closer.

'Ramos, back off!' Cage yelled, and he drew his six-gun and lifted it high for all to see.

Guthrie, a banker caught in a situation he was struggling to understand, hesitated fatally. Six-gun poised, he was distracted by that piercing cry. He half turned towards Cage, frowned, seemed to freeze. Cage gestured frantically, but had eyes only for Ramos and the other two Mexicans. He saw Ramos's crazy grin, the hypnotic flickering movement of the gleaming blade, saw his fierce companions move fast, closing on the banker. They were lunging in from the sides, filthy hands already clawing at Guthrie's arms. If they succeeded in holding him, Ramos would be free to come in from the front, thrusting and slashing, inflicting on the husband the same terrible wounds that had caused the death of his wife.

Without hesitation, Cage cocked his six-gun and planted a shot into the high ceiling.

The detonation was like a clap of thunder. As if swollen clouds had been pierced by a bolt of lightning, dust and cobwebs rained down. The man with the rusty Dragoon fell back against a table, bug-eyed, brought the heavy old pistol up and blasted a shot at Cage. The bullet flew high and wide, smacked into the far wall. The Mexican with the headband and eye patch ignored Cage and threw a wild punch at Guthrie's throat. The banker chopped at his head with his six-gun. The blow was softened by the headband, but not enough to stop the man's eyes from rolling. He hit the floor with a solid thump. Ramos's liquid black eyes flicked towards Guthrie, but his teeth flashed in a grin as he stepped in close and slashed with the knife. The banker's breath hissed. He stumbled back. His hand clutched at his throat where a thread of blood glistened bright red.

The Mexican Guthrie had struck was still down, groaning and spluttering through a mouthful of sawdust. The skinny man was again trying to bring the Dragoon to bear on Cage, but was driven backwards as Guthrie staggered. The banker's bloody fingers left his throat. He stretched out his arm, fighting for balance. His hand smeared the skinny Mexican's face with blood. Ramos was in close, but in no hurry to use his knife. Cage couldn't shoot, for fear of missing the 'breed and hitting the terrified banker.

The men at the bar had panicked at Cage's shot. Liquid splashed, glasses shattered, feet pounded as the drinkers ran for the doors and crashed noisily into the sunlit street. Those Mexican card players not intent on killing Guthrie had left the tables and scattered. Standing with their backs to the walls, they were ready to make a break for the door or the windows.

Then the barman moved in.

He'd started across the room at the first sign of trouble. Now he kicked a table out of the way and swung the big wooden stave with both hands. It hit the skinny Mexican's skull with a sound like an axe biting into a log. The Dragoon pistol flew from his hand. He collapsed in a boneless heap and lay still. Again the stave swished through the air. Ramos ducked, snarled something in Spanish and fell back. And now Guthrie was in the clear. Cage drew a bead on Ramos, but held his fire. A wild shot could down an innocent man — and if the barman had stopped the action why kill the 'breed?

Cage held back, shifted his position. He watched as Ramos allowed himself to be caught up in the rush as the Mexicans at last began running for the door and the safety of the street.

Then, from the door, two more warning shots rang out.

A deep voice yelled, 'Everybody stand still, don't nobody move.'

Marshal Frank Bellard had come in from the street. Accompanied by a tall deputy who had fired the warning shots, he was standing spread-legged, the badge shining on his vest, a six-gun cocked and held, barrel upwards, in his big fist.

Most of the Mexicans froze, rooted to the spot. As regulars in the Wayfarer, they would know Bellard; would know better than Cage the experienced lawman's deadly capabilities, and in any case had done no wrong. But for Ramos, a lawman represented the end of the line. He was a killer who knew arrest would lead swiftly to summary justice: if he wasn't lynched when news of his brutal crime got out, he would be tried, then legally hanged.

With his life at stake, Ramos took his only chance. He darted away from the crowd of Mexicans, took several long paces. Then he sprang. In mid-air he rolled himself into a ball and went through the window. To the sound of glass shattering and wood splintering he took with him the one big pane and most of the dry frame.

Guthrie watched him, grim-faced. Cage saw Bellard quickly appraise the situation in the saloon. The two Mexicans clubbed to the floor were stirring, groaning, but reluctant to rise while the barman hovered with his wooden stave. Bellard dismissed them with a glance, then snapped an order at his deputy. The tall man turned and left the saloon at a run.

Cage's concern now was for how Guthrie was going to react. His rage had focused on Ramos, but with Ramos gone would his anger be turned on Cage. Almost certainly — so Cage acted quickly to prevent the banker from making a big mistake. Stepping carelessly over the Mexican groaning on the floor, Cage winked at the barman and closed on the banker.

Guthrie looked away from the shattered window, and saw him coming.

Blood was running into his collar, but his face hardened and, sluggishly, he began to lift the six-gun.

But Cage was on him.

Without pause, he wrapped his arms around the banker, pushed his mouth close to his ear.

'If you want the man who murdered your wife,' he hissed, 'keep quiet.'

'Him, and you,' Guthrie gasped. 'That 'breed was with you, both of you are killers — '

'And this is my home territory. If you want the 'breed I can track him down, on your own you'll get nowhere — '

'What's going on, Cage?'

'This man is wounded, he needs a doctor,' Cage said quickly, and he turned to Frank Bellard, his face expressing concern. 'Guthrie, here, he saw the man who killed his wife, recklessly went for him and damn near paid for it with his life.'

'Ed Fitch has gone after that feller,' Bellard said, 'but I don't hold much hope. A man like that, a 'breed, he'll be across the river and on his own territory faster than you can spit.'

Cage looked at Guthrie, saw something in his eyes that told him the man was going to keep quiet, and cautiously released the man's arms. He took a half step away, then lifted the banker's chin with his curled finger and peered at the wound in his throat.

'It's all right,' he said, and saw the banker visibly relax, the apprehension fade from his eyes. 'You're bleeding like a stuck pig, but it's a shallow wound and you're not in any danger.'

'That's one of the reasons we put sawdust on the floor,' another, slightly husky voice chimed in, and Cage turned to meet the dark young woman's amused green eyes.

'Another is for the human trash that almost always ends up lying there at some time every day,' she said. 'Are you going to move these two sad cases, Frank, or should I get a couple of my boys to toss them in the alley?'

'Ed will be back from the river

shortly, empty handed,' Bellard said with resignation. 'He can throw a bucket of water over them, then walk 'em up to the jail. Meanwhile — '

'Meanwhile, this handsome fellow doesn't need a doctor,' the young woman said bluntly as she took hold of Guthrie's arm. 'If it's all right with you, I'll take him to my room and put a dressing on that scratch. That, and a shot of my best hooch, and he'll be as right as rain.'

'You do that, Vel,' the lawman said. 'And when he's all bandaged up, send him along to me. I'll be in my office asking Cage a lot of awkward questions to which, I'm quite sure, Mr Guthrie when he arrives can provide a lot of equally awkward answers.'

5

'I've no idea what went on in Drystone City,' Cage said, 'but I guess you could say I'm part responsible for what went on in the saloon.'

Bellard had his feet propped up on the desk. The jail's office smelt strongly of rich coffee. Cage found the room too warm for comfort, the blame for that down to the iron stove on which the coffee pot was bubbling. He'd opened the window overlooking the street, and placed his chair next to it. The breeze ruffled his dark hair.

'Responsible in what way?' Bellard said, firing up a cigarette.

'My trek home took me close to Drystone. Somewhere along the trail that 'breed who crashed out through the window tagged on to me, and we rode most of the way here together.'

'He do much talking?'

'I don't recollect anything about a bank robbery. Or a killing.'

'He may have arrived here hanging on to your coat tails, but you made recompense. From what I could see in the Wayfarer, you stepped in when that banker was in trouble. Was there some reason for doing that? Do you know the man?'

'Never seen him before today,' Cage said.

'You're sure about that?'

Cage nodded.

'Well, you're seeing him again now,' Bellard said, and he looked over as the door opened and Milton Guthrie walked in from the street.

For the next few minutes Cage listened with interest, and a degree of trepidation, as Guthrie introduced himself then sat back and with Bellard's full attention related the story of the attempted raid on his bank, from the moment two men broke into the house right through to when they rode out of Drystone City leaving him slumped by the hitch rail with a bullet wound in his shoulder.

'Only later,' he finished, 'did I discover that the man who had lingered in my house — that 'breed from the saloon — had cut my wife's throat.'

His voice cracked. Bellard cleared his throat, got up to splash coffee into three tin cups. When all three men were again settled, he looked at Cage.

'You must have been with that 'breed for, what, several days?'

'A week.'

'And still you can come up with nothing that might help Guthrie?'

'Nothing that would be of any use. The 'breed's a Mexican citizen. If you're right, and he's crossed the river, that leaves you and every other lawman on this side of the border with their hands tied.'

'It's not lawmen that man should fear,' Milton Guthrie said, his voice tight.

'Going after him yourself is not something I would advise,' Bellard said.

'But he had a companion in crime,' and, as he spoke, he looked directly at Cage. He let the words gather portent, then switched his gaze to Guthrie. 'That man, was he white?'

'Yes.'

'And would you know him if you saw him again?'

'Oh yes,' Guthrie said, and he too flashed a glance at Cage. 'He stood up against me in our bedroom, threatened me, punched me in the mouth. He may not have wielded the knife, but both those villains are equally guilty.'

'Then I think there lies your best hope,' Bellard said. 'If he remains in Mexico the 'breed is beyond the reach of United States law. But if the other man can be found, then he could be brought to justice.' He looked at the smouldering end of his cigarette, thought for a moment, then smiled as if secretly amused. 'Cage poked his nose in to good effect in the saloon. He might be willing to help you in your hunt for this second man.'

Guthrie glowered at Cage, and opened his mouth. But before he could utter one damning word, Cage lifted a cautionary hand.

'If we join forces,' Cage said, 'we could help each other. My brother's missing, and he's under a cloud of suspicion. I need to find him, get to the truth, then clear his name. But I'm also going renegade hunting. Mexican rustlers burnt down my parents' house when they were asleep in their bed. They both died in the fire.'

It took a while for Guthrie to answer, and Cage could follow his thoughts without any difficulty. Guthrie would be fiercely opposed to offering help of any kind to Cage. But common sense would be telling him that if Cage could help hunt down the 'breed who had murdered his wife, the offer should be snapped up. After all, there would be nothing to stop him turning his wrath on Cage once Ramos was behind bars, or lying riddled with bullets in the Mexican scrub.

'If you are going after those murdering Mexicans,' Guthrie said at last, 'then you'll be crossing the river? If I agree to help you — '

'Ramos will be one of our targets,' Cage finished for him.

'This,' Bellard said thoughtfully, 'sounds like the makings of a plan. By rights, as town marshal, I should advise you to leave the hunting down of criminals to officers of the law.' Then he shook his head. 'Oh, hell, listen, I'm rambling on again . . . Look, I'll give you just one word of warning: take great care. That Ramos feller is sure to have crossed the river to join up with some old pals, and they're as likely as not to be *bandidos*. Fierce bastards, cut your throat as soon as look at you.'

'Maybe the same ones who burned down the Butlers' house,' Cage said with sudden optimism. 'If Ramos is in with that mob, then we're looking at killing two birds with one stone.'

6

The day was all worn out.

After agreeing with a surly Guthrie to meet at the livery barn soon after dawn the next day, Cage crossed the street from the jail office to the Alhambra Hotel and booked himself a room for the night. Then he strolled back down the street to a café situated opposite the Wayfarer — now boasting a shattered window — and worked his way through a heaped plate of steak and eggs washed down with strong coffee while idly watching the dark-haired young woman from the saloon. She was out on the plankwalk, her pale yellow dress liquid gold in the late evening sun, berating a swamper who was making hard work of sweeping up the broken glass.

Quite a gal, Cage thought. What had Bellard called her? Vel? Now, what was that short for? Had the marshal got it wrong, or had Cage misheard? Had he really said Val, which would be short for Valerie and still a name that was unfamiliar?

And then, out of nowhere, a vision came floating out of Cage's past and he was up in a tree watching a young girl with short plaits, down by the wide river, holding up her long skirts and squealing in delight as she splashed barefoot through the shallows in the rain.

Not exactly his childhood sweetheart, but for a time there they'd been inseparable . . .

Velvet Goodwine, that was her name. Her father, Erskine, was a widower, and he owned the Wayfarer. But he'd been a white-haired old man then, thirty years or more ago and, by the time Cage left town, Erskine was limping painfully down into the saloon rarely, and then only to fix his nervous manager with his eagle eye, keep him up on his toes and dancing to the saloonist's tune.

Erskine had passed on, Cage mused.

The manager must have wearied and given way to the old man's daughter — and, from what Cage had seen, she had slipped into the role of saloon keeper as easily as a duck to water.

But there had been a man with her at the bar, a senior figure businesslike in his demeanour, his gaze supercilious. Perhaps he was the new owner, Velvet Goodwine the previous owner's daughter relegated to barmaid duties, a splash of colour and feminine allure for the clientéle to ogle while buying drinks.

And yet it hadn't looked that way when Ramos had made his break and the dust had settled. It was the woman who had taken control, saying something to Bellard about her boys tossing the dazed Mexicans into the alley — and the distinguished businessman with the silver hair and the ostentatious gold watch chain had been notable only by his absence . . .

Cage pushed his plate away, lit a cigarette, then sat back and, not for the first time, wondered what the hell he was letting himself in for by lining up with Milton Guthrie. The banker was a man torn by grief, consumed by anger and hatred for not one man, but two. In the days to come Cage was going to be alone on the trail with a man who must surely want him dead. There would be times when his back would be turned to a man Bellard said 'had enough weaponry hooked on belt and saddle to equip an army'. Which would, no doubt, come in mighty handy if they fell foul of a bunch of grinning Mexican renegades, but wasn't likely to be of much comfort to Cage when he lay in his blankets fighting sleep while a vengeful Guthrie toyed with a six-gun by the camp-fire.

But first things first, and before they began hunting Mexicans on their own territory there was the small matter of Matt Butler. According to John Lawrence, Matt was holed up in the Butler line cabin. The look Lawrence had thrown at Cage in his office suggested that Frank Bellard was ignorant of that fact. So, make sure Bellard's back was turned, and ride out to talk to Matt.

Cage chuckled, letting smoke spill from his lips.

Never had known what label to pin on Matt Butler. Adoptive brother had always seemed . . . well . . . cold-blooded? Brother was the obvious choice, but during school days calling Matt that had always drawn catcalls and derision. In the knowing eyes of all the other kids, Matt Butler and Cage were unrelated, Cage the young stranger who had walked boldly out of the wilderness to stake a claim to which he had no entitlement.

What I should call Matt now, Cage thought, his face sobering as thoughts returned to the present, is a damned fool. And then that sounded ridiculous even to Cage's own ears, because if Matt Butler was a fool for robbing a bank to help the blood-parents he could see fading with every hard day that passed, then what was he, Cage? He had tried exactly the same damn fool trick two years ago when Matt had first appealed for money. No reason given. Just the hand held out over the miles, and Cage had jumped. Straight into a prison cell. And even that had taught him nothing, because two years later the call had come again, and . . .

Out on the street, angry with himself, he flicked his cigarette away in the gathering gloom, and turned towards the hotel. As he made his way towards the Alhambra, and the single room that would be his to rest in until dawn broke, he couldn't hold back a flicker of amusement.

Tomorrow they would begin a three-way search. John Lawrence had pointed the way towards Matt — but that was the only definite information they had, and that search anyway was a distraction from their real mission.

Guthrie wanted Ramos, Cage the men who had set a Texas ranch house alight and left an ageing couple to perish in the raging fire. But in Mexico, they could lose themselves among the simple peasants tending their flocks or tilling the soil. They would be difficult to find, almost impossible to catch.

So Cage thought as he headed for his room. Within hours he would discover that his thinking was flawed — and it would prove to be a costly mistake.

7

They had covered less than ten miles when Guthrie became convinced they were being followed.

After picking up their horses from the barn, dew glistening on the rickety windmill that supplied water for the town's horse trough and their white breath mingling with a river mist that hung at window level all the way down the main street, they'd ridden out of town in a northerly direction before leaving the trail to follow the grassy river-bank.

In the first few miles, as the sun began warming the air, Cage told Guthrie what had happened to his adoptive parents; mostly for something to talk about, because Guthrie maintained a sullen silence, but also to get it clear in his own mind. Then, because talking about a Texas ranch might have painted an erroneous image in Guthrie's imagination, Cage explained some more.

The Butler spread, Cage told him, comprised a few hundred acres stretching inland from the river some fifteen miles north of Nathan's Ford. When Al Butler stocked the land and built the house he'd thought giving the place any name other than his own would be pretentious, so that's what it had always remained: the Butler spread; one man's attempt — again in Al's words — to scratch a living from the soil in the way most favoured by the terrain and climate of the region.

'He stayed small,' Cage said, 'because if he could feed his family and manage to put some cash in the bank, Al didn't see any need to bust a gut. So there he was, working a small spread stuck midway between town and the prosperous Flanagan ranch to the north, but not close enough to either of them to be protected from the trouble inflicted by certain humans in these parts.' Cage shot a glance at the banker. 'Most bad men know when there are easy pickings to be had, so I'd say it was pretty obvious where rustlers coming out of Mexico would strike.'

And that was when Guthrie said, 'There's someone on our tail.'

'Yeah, and you'd know that for sure,' Cage said caustically, 'you a man used to sitting on his backside, all day and every day, behind a nice shiny desk.'

'Please yourself.'

Cage twisted in the saddle, looked back. 'You're right, I shouldn't have said that. Even a man working in an office is born with eyes and ears. So, what did you see?'

'I heard what I think was a horse whinnying. I glanced over my shoulder. There's a prominent stand of trees a mile or so back. We rode around it, on the river side. I saw movement on the fringe of those trees — then it was gone. Also, there's some tell-tale dust.'

'Dust hangs,' Cage said. 'Could be ours.'

'Yes.'

'Or not.'

'Why did you try to rob my bank?'

The question came at him like a shot. Caught unawares, Cage shrugged, searched for an answer.

'The first time I tried a stunt like that,' he said, 'I made a mess of it and ended up spending a couple of years in jail. Al, my pa, had always drilled into me that practise makes perfect.' He gazed ahead, half smiling. 'Obviously, I'm not getting enough of that. You think I should persist?'

He could feel Guthrie looking hard at him, not taking the question seriously, clearly puzzled.

'I just don't understand — ' Guthrie broke off, shook his head. 'As a banker I have to be a shrewd judge of character. One look at that — '

'Ramos.'

'Ramos, yes, one look at him and I know exactly where I stand, I can see violence and treachery in the man. I wouldn't trust him with your money, never mind mine.'

'I lived with him for a year,' Cage said, 'and still don't know him.'

Guthrie shook his head irritably. 'His kind are shallow, once below the surface there's nothing to know, but you . . . '

'We all have reasons for what we do,' Cage said softly, his eyes looking ahead to the blackened ruins that were all that was left of what had been a pretty ranch house nestling in a hollow between river and trees. 'If you look where I'm looking, you'll see all that remains of mine.'

* * *

There was nothing they could do at the house where Cage had spent his early years. A small cluster of outbuildings across the yard had escaped the blaze, but they were small compensation. After a slow ride past that saw the horses' hoofs kicking up a choking black dust around the untouched outbuildings, they turned away and cut inland in a north-easterly direction.

Once they were on the trail, Cage maintained a watchful silence, Guthrie slipped into a pensive mood. The banker's wife had died, he had been left bereft, and for that someone must pay. Two men had been responsible for the crime. The only one within range of Guthrie's weapons was Cage. He was watching his back.

They rode for thirty minutes under a sun that was becoming uncomfortably hot. The grass was parched. Dust kicked up by the horses saw both men pulling up bandannas to cover their faces, leaving their eyes to squint ahead as best they could. What lay in front of them was seemingly endless grassland, becoming more undulating as they left the river behind. The monotonous landscape was relieved here and there by stands of trees marking those locations where, over the years, the run-off from winter rains had collected in hollows. The acres in the immediate vicinity were those where Al Butler's cattle had once grazed, while the vast expanse of open range as far north as they could see belonged to the big Flanagan ranch.

Because they rode in silence the sudden crackle of gunfire was all the more startling. Both men were snapped out of their reverie. Guthrie was visibly shocked. His head snapped around. He was looking to the north, his eyes searching wildly. A second shot cracked. It was followed by another, then a rattling volley.

'Damn it,' Cage said, lifting his hand to gaze into the sun, 'that gunfire's coming from somewhere close to where we're heading; the line cabin lies over in that direction.'

'What line cabin?'

'The Butler cabin where my brother's hiding.'

'Now hold on a minute. I distinctly heard you tell Bellard you were setting out to *find* your brother.'

'Well, now we have,' Cage said

laconically, touching spurs to the roan. 'Trouble is, so's someone else, and if that was Matt pulling the trigger I'd say he's not too pleased.'

They set out across the range, their horses at a dead run, Cage in front and cutting away at an angle towards a higher rise where a line of trees was outlined against the sky.

'That person I thought I saw earlier,' Guthrie said, forcing his horse level, gasping, breathless with the effort.

'Yes. Suddenly takes on significance. I think whoever it was must have gone straight past when we were wasting time at the ruins,' Cage said. 'My guess is it's Bellard himself, acting cagey, or maybe his deputy — '

'Ed Fitch.'

'Yeah, one or the other. Followed us for a while, saw the direction we were taking and put two and two together.'

'What sort of trouble's your brother in?'

Cage flashed Guthrie a fierce grin, his hat brim flattened, the bandanna slipped down from his face leaving his teeth bared.

'I believe he tried to rob a bank.'

Guthrie looked stunned.

A breeze was ruffling the longer dry grass so that the two men had the impression of riding hock-deep through a moving ocean. The shadows from high clouds floating across the rippling surface were disorientating, intensifying the illusion.

They had covered a fast half mile, and Cage had just spotted the line cabin, when the first shot hissed over their heads like an angry hornet. Cage ducked. The second shot sliced through the air where his head had been, a third hummed closer to Guthrie as the unseen gunman shifted aim.

Neither of the shots had been fired from the cabin, a drab building with a tin chimney poking through the shingle roof, almost invisible against a back-drop of grey-green cottonwoods. Cage had seen no muzzle flash, no tell-tale drift of smoke, and he wondered if Matt had moved up to the tree-lined higher ground some way behind the cabin when he caught sight of the approaching rider.

Then that idea seemed to have been knocked on the head when a rifle cracked from a stand of trees away to the cabin's left — and at the same time Cage spotted a horse in a shallow hollow a hundred yards to the right of their line of approach, and knew they had found the cause of all the excitement.

'Over there,' he called to Guthrie, and pointed to the horse.

They raced for the cover of that low ground. Several shots winged harmlessly overhead. Then they were over the depression's lip and tumbling from the saddle.

'Warning shots,' Cage gasped as they fell to the ground on the slope below the rim. 'Don't come any closer is what they're telling us.'

'Warning shots with the clear intent to kill or maim,' Guthrie pointed out with commendable perception. 'I'd say there's at least two out there, both shooting with the aim of dropping men where they stand.'

'And the one over in the trees is a Mexican.'

Cage snapped his head around to look up the slope. He'd spotted the horse, now he was looking at the man. It was Ed Fitch who had made the comment. The tall deputy was hunkered down, his head below the line of fire where white rocks poked through the grass and moss on the hollow's lip. A bloodstained bandanna was wrapped around his left forearm. His lean face was scratched. His rifle was pointing directly at Cage. There was a look on his face that told of his chagrin: in a secure position that made him reasonably safe from the distant riflemen, he had left himself exposed at the rear.

'Bellard send you after me?' Cage said.

Fitch shook his head, then ducked

down and grimaced as a bullet chipped sharp fragments from a rock and howled off into the distance.

'My idea — and it's turned out to be a bad one, maybe the last I'll ever have.' He rose to fire a quick shot at an unseen target, then ducked down again and stared hard at Cage.

'That's your brother out there. Why didn't you shoot me in the back as you rode up?'

'Don't be a damn fool. I'm here to help him, not commit murder.'

'I had a word with Velvet Goodwine. She'd recognized you right off.'

'And she told you where Matt was holed up?'

'No, sir. That's the one thing she would not do. But she told me all about your good self. Knows what you've been doing, in particular the last three or four years. I tell you, going by the tale she tells you don't strike me as a law-abiding, peaceable man.'

Cage flashed a quick glance at

Guthrie, met his impassive gaze, looked back at Fitch.

'So you followed us from town, worked out where Matt had to be from the direction we took?'

Fitch nodded. 'Yeah, I worked that out, but ran into trouble.'

Cage moved up to the rim and peered out between the boulders. He did it impulsively, without caution. A bullet chipped a sharp sliver of stone into his cheek. It stung like red-hot iron. He clapped a hand to his face. It came away stained red. The wasted lead whined skywards. It was followed by the flat crack of the rifle. Cage cursed, slid back from the rim. He glanced across at Fitch.

'Who's the Mexican?'

'He's been working for Al Butler,' Fitch said. He lifted the rifle, thoughtfully ran his hand along the hot barrel, stared hard at Cage. 'If I poke my head up, it gets shot off. Same almost happened to you. You're as much at risk as I am, and the hot reception you got when you rode in should come as no surprise. The Mex doesn't know you, your brother hasn't seen you since you were a kid of eighteen.'

'They're too far off to tell one man from another anyway,' Guthrie said.

Fitch shook his head. 'Only partly true. They know me, would recognize my horse, the way I ride, and they know I represent the law. What I'm saying is, they had me pinned down, then two men rode in to help. They see us as tarred with the same brush.'

Guthrie glanced at Cage. 'You could try shouting. Holler real loud, let them know you're kin, not law.'

'They'd suspect a trick,' Cage said. 'And they're holding all the cards. We're pinned down, with no way out of this damned hollow.'

'But I'm going to give it a try,' Fitch said, 'and if I can make it without picking up a lump of hot lead — '

He let the words hang. Without waiting to see if Cage was going to argue he slid down from the rim. He ran at a half crouch, made it to his horse, slid the rifle into its boot and threw himself into the saddle. Instantly, his move was spotted by the distant gunmen. Rifles opened up from the high timber, and from the trees to the left of the line cabin.

At another time, in different circumstances, Cage thought, he'd have suggested to Guthrie that the two of them crawled to the rim and sent a hail of lead in the direction of the unseen gunmen to cover Fitch's getaway. But it was Cage's brother out there, and covering fire intended only to keep heads down had been known to kill.

So, instead of assisting in any way, Cage watched and cringed as bullets aimed at Fitch hit the rocks and howled into the clear skies, or whined across the hollow carrying death's sinister whisper close enough for the deputy to see the shadow of the grim reaper. And it was with the threat of death uncomfortably close to his ears that Fitch flattened himself along the horse's neck and spurred recklessly out of the hollow.

He rode flat out, swinging wide and making use of what timber there was for flimsy cover. The trees provided little protection, but made it difficult for the gunmen to track their prey. Cage watched Fitch's progress, the flicker of light and shade across horse and rider that provided the gunmen with an impossible target. When the trees ran out, leaving Fitch exposed, he was several hundred yards from the hollow, and already out of accurate rifle range. The guns fell silent. Within minutes Fitch was nothing more than a dot, shimmering and dancing in the heat-haze.

'Mark my words,' Cage said softly, 'Matt will read more into what he's just seen than a man fleeing for his life.'

'My thoughts exactly,' Guthrie said. 'If one man leaves in a hurry and two remain, there can be but one reason.'

'Fitch has gone to get help.' Cage pulled a face, looked at Guthrie. 'In those circumstances, what would you do?'

'Get the hell out of here,' Guthrie said. 'And fast.'

Cage wriggled back to the rim, squinted out between the rocks. Then he swore, stood up and cupped his hands to his mouth.

'Matt!' he roared. 'Matt, it's Cage . . . '

He listened to his voice fall away, deadened by heat and distance, dying without any hope of reaching the two gunmen. And Cage had shouted out of desperation, for his hasty glance between the rocks had told him that Matt and the Mexican were already beating a retreat. A horseman had come hammering down from the high trees, too far away to recognize. He joined the rider emerging from the timber to the left of the cabin, and both were now galloping away in a westerly direction.

'Gone,' Cage said. Rejoining Guthrie, he ripped off his Stetson and flung it angrily to the ground. 'An hour from now they'll be across the Rio Grande and losing themselves in Mexico.'

He heard a grunt of acknowledgement, and saw a smile twitching the banker's lips. The bereaved man had seen something amusing in what, to Cage, had turned out to be a complete waste of time.

'What's funny?'

'Not funny, ironic. You came here to talk to your brother; you also want to find the men who murdered your parents, and I want Ramos. The only way we can get what we want now is by crossing into Mexico, which is what we should have done in the first place.'

'Mexico's a big country.'

'That's why what we do next is head back to Nathan's Ford. Remember what Fitch told you? He spoke to Velvet Goodwine. She was able to tell him a lot about you, about what you've been doing the past few years.' He paused. 'How could she know all that?'

Cage frowned. 'Beats me. But why does it matter?'

'You were in the Wayfarer when Ramos made his break. Maybe you were too busy watching me — I don't know, but I saw something that escaped your notice.'

'Go on.'

'Velvet Goodwine knows Ramos, and knows him well. She called something to him. I didn't catch it, but it sounded like she was throwing some good advice his way. The next thing, Ramos is out of the window.' Guthrie paused again, looked at Cage. 'You knew Velvet when you were a young boy, but the reason we're riding to Nathan's Ford is because the only link between you and her — as adults — is that knife murdering 'breed, Ramos.'

8

They timed it so that they rode back into town when the sun had settled for the night beneath the blanket of red and gold covering the western hills. In the warm half light of early evening, specks of light flared as matches were applied to the oil lamps hanging over the mostly deserted plankwalks.

'Book a couple of rooms in the Alhambra,' Cage said, as they drew level with the hotel. 'I was figuring on spending just the one night here, but that could change. I'll know more when I've spoken to Velvet, but I think it's best if I see her alone.'

Guthrie nodded, and peeled away. He was tying his horse at the hotel's hitch rail when Cage pushed on past John Lawrence's office — a light glowing in the window — and rode through the big double doors and down the wide runway of Elliott's livery barn. He'd decided to place the roan in the expert care of the town's hostler, preparation for the hard work the horse would surely have to do if they did cross into Mexico. Elliott — an old, lame man who'd been a wrangler most of his life — listened to Cage's request, nodded, spat, took Cage's silver coins and the reins of his roan.

When Cage strode back towards the street, the roan's saddle was already off and draped over a rail, and he was smiling in wonder at the old hostler's efficiency when he walked out into the fresh air.

Then the hostler was forgotten as his thoughts drifted ahead to the dark-haired woman who was across the street in the Wayfarer. A businesswoman, almost certainly the saloon's owner, yet, inexplicably, she was a woman who numbered among her acquaintances the murdering half-breed who had shared a cell with Cage. And was intimate enough with him, it seemed, to have had conversations in which Cage had figured prominently.

The distraction caused by his thoughts on the unexpected complication was Cage's undoing. He almost collided with a tall, grey-haired man with sharp blue eyes who was leading a horse towards the barn. He was coming around the horse trough, saying something over his shoulder to Marshal Frank Bellard.

When he faced front, he saw Cage. Recognition was instant — for both men; the stranger was Marshal Dave Eyke of Drystone City.

'Goddammit, that's him,' Eyke shouted — and he released the reins and brought a clean, hard punch up from somewhere by his hip. It caught Cage on the angle of his jaw. He saw a flicker of red, then a shower of stars, staggered on legs turned into wet string. Eyke grabbed his shoulder, swung him around and hit him again. This time the punch struck Cage dead centre. Agony shot through his head.

He felt his nose crunch. Blood gushed. Tears filled his eyes. Eyke's horse panicked, reared, then kicked out. A flailing hoof grazed Cage's skull. Then he was staggering back against the trough. He hit the rim hard with the backs of his thighs and plunged into the rank water.

Eyke used both hands to grab him by his soaked shirt. He lifted Cage clear of the stinking water, dragged him roughly back over the trough's rim and dumped him on the ground. Cage's head cracked against the rock-hard surface. He was half under the trough. He coughed, spat blood and water, then swung a wild, sweeping kick at Eyke. It connected and took the marshal's feet from under him. He roared in rage as he fell. The cry was choked off. He fell awkwardly. The impact drove the breath from his lungs.

Cage rolled on to his knees. He shook his head, blood spraying. Bellard had rushed in to take hold of Eyke's terrified horse. One hand was gripping the bunched reins up near the bit. He was fighting the heavy animal, using his shoulder but lurching off balance. At the same time he was fumbling for his six-gun.

Gripping the trough with one hand, Cage regained his feet. He stood, wobbling, dragged a sleeve across his face to clear blood and tears. Eyke was on his way up, gasping. His blue eyes were fixed on Cage, his mouth twisted in rage. He came upright, reached for his six-gun. It was a smooth, fast draw. Again Cage kicked out. His toe cracked against Eyke's wrist. The six-gun went spinning into the air.

'That will do!'

Frank Bellard snapped the order. He'd released Eyke's horse. The animal had fled up the street, knocking aside a curious onlooker. Freed of that encumbrance, the Ford's marshal had both feet firmly braced, both hands free. His six-gun was out and levelled at Cage.

Then another voice rang out, loud, clear and with a degree of authority.

'What the hell's going on here?'

It was Milton Guthrie.

An oil lamp creaked on rusty brackets as a breeze picked up. A door banged open and men came swarming out of the saloon. Men and women had appeared from nowhere and were watching from the opposite plankwalk. Others, like the man bowled over by the horse, had crossed the street and were edging close. The hostler, Vern Elliott, was watching from his barn. Cage could see the deputy, Fitch, outlined in the light flooding from the jail's door.

Dave Eyke was bent over, clutching his wrist, his gun yards away. Bellard stood with his gun levelled, but was looking back and frowning as Guthrie walked across to Cage. Cage nodded to him. He was standing in a pool of water, his face a mask of blood. Guthrie touched his shoulder, shook his head.

Eyke coughed, straightened.

'That man is one of the fellers who tried to rob your bank, Milt.'

'He's the man who tried to rob my

bank, if I say so,' Milton Guthrie said. 'If I say nothing — what then?'

'Christ, what the hell are you talking about?'

'Priorities. What matters most to me. I followed two men across country for seven days. One of those men murdered my wife.'

'Both of them entered your house. One punched you in the face.'

'You only have my word for that. Could be I tripped and fell — '

'We stood in the street, early hours, outside your bank. You told me exactly what had happened. And you know what happened next. There was gunplay. I was pinned in a doorway, you took a slug in the shoulder. You were down on your knees when the 'breed who plugged you stole your horse and rode out of town.' Eyke jerked a thumb at Cage. 'This feller got away through the alley alongside your bank. What you're saying now is a contradiction. It makes no sense, and is beyond my understanding.'

'There's been seven days' hard riding between then and now,' Guthrie said, 'me following two men, careful not to be seen. That's given me time to think. Upon reflection, I'd say this man has committed no offence for which he can be charged — '

'He discharged his pistol at an officer of the law.'

'If that's what happened, he missed.' Guthrie smiled. 'In the end all he did was drill holes in a door frame. At most, that warrants a night in a cell to cool off. As for the other, without my word you have no shred of proof that he tried to rob my bank.'

'Goddammit, Milt,' Eyke said hoarsely, but Guthrie, holding Cage's shoulder and leading him away, silenced him with a fierce glare.

'It's down to priorities, Dave. All you or I need to know about this man, Cage, is that starting tomorrow morning he's going to help me hunt down the man who entered my wife's bedroom and cut her throat.'

9

Velvet Goodwine stepped back. The gauze in her hand was red with blood. With head tilted and amusement lurking in her dark eyes, she looked critically at Cage.

'It's not broken,' she said, 'though that punch has probably ruined your looks for a while.'

'I wasn't born handsome so I couldn't care less, but right now my whole face is a mass of pain.'

'You'll live.'

'To fight another day? Well, that's as it should be, because three men crossed the river and I'm going after two of them for reasons that are different but of equal importance.'

'You talk educated, Cage. Did you study books while you were in prison?'

He gave her a calculating look. 'Fitch said he'd talked to you. Said you know more about me than I know myself, and it seems he was right.'

'Don't believe him. I got snippets of news from time to time, that's all.' She rinsed the gauze in a basin of hot water, began bathing his face.

'You know I've been in jail. D'you know why?'

'You robbed a bank in southern Texas.'

'Almost died in the attempt, but that's all it was: wasted effort, a foolish try that didn't work out.'

'Really?' She stepped back, looked at his wet face, patted it with a dry cloth. 'Then it's a great pity Matt didn't hear about the failure.'

He pushed her hand away, stood up. 'You told him what I'd done?'

She shook her head. 'Not me, no, but he knew all about it. Goodness, why do you think he tried the same fool trick? His thinking was, if Cage can do it, so can I.'

'I don't understand any of this. I've been miles away from my home, long enough to grow from childhood to manhood — if I can call it that,' he said ruefully. 'In the later years Matt sent wires several times, pleading with me for money. Those wires caught up with me, eventually. I read them all, and one sounded so desperate I decided I had to act. The result was failure, as you know. But I never replied to those wires, not once — yet somehow you know I've been in jail, you know why, and so does Matt.'

They were in the room behind the saloon. It was a living-room, and the feminine touches told Cage it was where Velvet lived. She'd moved away from him and was leaning back against the table. The pale-yellow dress had been changed for one of deep red that covered her from neck to ankles. Ideal for mopping up blood, Cage thought, and gingerly touched his nose.

Velvet said, watching him, 'An outlaw's deeds would be splashed across the newspapers. Those papers would be freely available to people far and wide.'

'No.' He shook his head. 'I'm a failed bank robber, not Jesse James. You heard about me, but it wasn't from anything sensational written by a jobbing journalist.'

'Do you know Sergio Aguera?'

He shook his head.

'He worked for your father.' She lifted an eyebrow, waited.

'Ah.' Cage nodded slowly. 'Fitch had something to say about that when three of us were pinned down in a hollow near the Butler line cabin. Aguera must be the Mexican who a few hours ago was looking at me over the sights of a rifle.'

'Whatever he did out there would have been out of loyalty to your family. You were a stranger, he would have been doing his best to protect Matt.'

'And would happily have killed me if that's what it took,' Cage said, nodding impatiently. 'Is there a point in this?'

'Sergio Aguera has a half-brother who's a couple of years older,' Velvet said. 'The father — mixed race — died soon after that first boy was born. His mother remarried a pure-blood Mexican called Carlos Aguera and they had a second son.' She waited, let that register. When there was no response, she said, 'If you really did educate yourself during those hours in a cell, surely you can work out where this is leading?'

For a moment there was silence. Then Cage's eyes widened, and he said, very softly, 'That first son was Pepe Ramos.'

'You see? And, unlike you, Ramos did write letters from his prison cell.'

'From our cell. We did hard time together.'

Velvet nodded understanding. 'There you are. That's how Ramos knows so much about you. In the letters he wrote he passed that knowledge on to his younger half-brother, Sergio Aguera, because obviously — unlike you — he knew of the connection: his half-brother was working for your family. It was Aguera who gave all the news to Matt.

But whenever he was in town, Aguera also talked to me. I've known both of them for years, Sergio Aguera and Pepe Ramos. In fact, I got Sergio the job with your father. Al Butler was in here one day and asked me if I knew of anyone looking for work. I recommended Sergio.'

'And here's me thinking Ramos was a stranger here, that he came to the Ford hanging on to my coat tails.'

Velvet shook her head. 'Maybe he did do that, but he's no stranger. Because his half-brother was working for your father, Pepe often came across the river, and the two of them would drink in here.' She paused, reflecting. 'Pepe felt at home in the Wayfarer. He spent so much time in here, if you go out there now you'll probably make out the grooves his elbows left in the bar.'

'Pepe Ramos,' Cage said, 'is a cold-blooded killer.'

'I'll believe that when I see proof,' said Velvet Goodwine flatly.

'Unfortunately, that might prove difficult.'

Cage swung around. The door had clicked open. A man had entered the room. White hair, dark suit, the glittering gold of a looped watch chain. Last seen, Cage realized, standing at the bar alongside Velvet when Guthrie had gone after Ramos and all hell had broken loose.

'The woman's dead, throat cut from ear to ear,' Cage told him. 'Her husband found her. Ramos was the last man with her.'

'Ah, but that's the bit that cannot be proved. You and Guthrie left the banker's house, a few minutes later Ramos emerged. But the three of you then rode into Drystone City, and it was some hours later when Guthrie returned home to discover his wife's dead body. If it went to trial, any good lawyer working for Ramos would suggest that the woman was alive when he left. He'd argue that marauders could have entered the house during

Guthrie's lengthy absence.'

Cage frowned, searching his memory. 'I walked out of the house with Guthrie. When Ramos followed he was waving a bottle of whiskey. His knife . . . ?' He shrugged. 'OK, maybe somebody else walked in and murdered Guthrie's wife. But the only way I'll get to know for sure is by looking into Pepe Ramos's eyes and asking the question.'

'But Ramos is in Mexico,' Velvet said.

'I'll help Guthrie find him. We're crossing the river at dawn.'

'But there's more, isn't there?' Velvet said.

'Of course. Matt crossing over came as a complete surprise. My main intention all along has been to hunt down the Mexican rustlers who murdered my parents.'

Velvet frowned. 'What makes you so sure Matt's over there?'

'He lit out from the line cabin when I was pinned down with Guthrie and it looked certain Fitch was running to town for a posse. Aguera was with

Matt. The border was within spitting distance.'

'Then I'll go with you.'

Cage stared in astonishment at Velvet Goodwine.

'This is Alan Spence,' she went on, nodding at the big man. 'My apologies for not introducing him earlier. Alan's a businessman with pots of money and he has an interest in the Wayfarer. Not financial, at least, not at present' — she smiled across at Spence — 'but I'm quite sure he'd be willing to supervise the management of the place while I'm away.'

'You have no idea how dangerous this could turn out to be,' Spence said.

'Lucky you. If anything happens to me, then you've got yourself a saloon,' Velvet said. 'But I'll be quite safe. I've known Mexicans all my life, I speak the language, know their customs, their ways.'

'But what about this man, Cage, fresh out of jail? About him you know nothing.'

'I grew up with him. What's the Biblical saying? 'Give me the child until he is seven, I'll give you the man'? I knew him at that age, and for some time afterwards.'

'But not now. I'm expressing concern because the information I got came from a long talk with Frank Bellard and Marshal Dave Eyke from Drystone City. Eyke's gone home — he left an inexperienced deputy in charge. But when Cage and Pepe Ramos were in Guthrie's house demanding the keys to his bank, there was violence. Most of it was administered by Cage's fists. Later, in town, Ramos and Cage escaped by turning their guns on Eyke.'

'I knew nothing of that,' Velvet said, 'but from what he and I have been discussing I know Cage must have been motivated by a need to help his elderly parents.'

'You're naïve, and much too trusting. But even if you're right, there's still the killer, Ramos.'

'You want to do two things,' Cage

said angrily. 'The first is stop talking about me as if I'm not here in the same room. The other is to make up your damn mind about Ramos. A few minutes ago you were suggesting someone else killed Guthrie's wife.'

'I'm interested in Velvet's welfare.'

'What you're interested in,' Velvet Goodwine said, 'is a saloon called the Wayfarer. Well, for the next several days she's all yours, Alan, because as from tomorrow morning the owner will be across the river hunting bandits in Mexico.'

10

'I never did cross the river, even as a boy,' Cage said. 'I seem to recall your pa taking you over when you were a little girl, Velvet Goodwine.'

'You mean when you and I were sweet on each other?'

Cage felt himself colour.

'What I mean is those early trips may have given you a fondness for the land. If you've been across more recently you'll likely have an idea where the nearer pueblos are located, and so I'm mighty pleased you came along for the ride.'

'You think that's what this is? A constitutional to take the morning air? Well, let me tell you, Cage, I don't know what truth there is in Alan Spence's story, but one of the reasons I'm here is to stand between you two and Pepe Ramos.'

'That's for you and Cage to work out,' Milt Guthrie said, and there was a thread of anger tightening his voice. 'I don't hold with violence of any kind, but I'd advise both of you to stay well out of my way when we find that 'breed.'

The early morning sun was low in the east, scarcely warming their backs as they rode through the hanging river mist. Glittering droplets were still being flung from the legs of their mounts. The riders had only moments ago taken the trail out of Nathan's Ford and rattled over the stony crossing that had given the town its name — usable only at certain times, and even then deep enough for the water to reach stirrups and wash over boots — and urged their horses up the steep bank and so into the state of Coahuila, Mexico.

Both men were dressed in rough range garb, wore belted six-guns and had Winchester rifles tucked into leather boots, butts forward. In their saddle-bags they carried water bottles, jerky and biscuits, and spare ammunition for pistols and long guns.

Velvet Goodwine was, in Cage's opinion, a feast for the eyes. Away from the false glitter of the Wayfarer saloon she had jettisoned the vivid frocks she usually wore in favour of dark trousers and a blouse of the deepest red that was cut loose for comfort. Her long dark hair was tied back in a ponytail that reached almost to her waist, and her flat-crowned black hat was tilted at a rakish angle.

However, the picture of delectable and fragile feminine pulchritude finished there. Around her waist was buckled a belt carrying a British Beaumont Adams revolver — her father, Reg Goodwine, had been an English immigrant — the butt of a Spencer carbine protruded from the boot under her right leg, and Cage recalled with considerable admiration that Velvet had begun firing both handguns and rifles from a very early age. She had been taught well, by a father who knew he would not always be there to protect the daughter who was destined to mature into a beautiful, desirable woman living in a wild, untamed land.

Velvet caught Cage watching her, and stuck out her tongue. Just as she used to do when they were children, he remembered. He looked away quickly, feeling his pulse stir, led the way at a steady canter for a further hundred yards or so then eased his mount back to a slow walk.

Again he spoke to Velvet.

'During our time inside I got a name from Ramos: the pueblo where he was born. If I remember correctly it's a place called San Luis. Does that ring a bell?'

Velvet nodded. 'It's a small village on a hillside, some twenty miles to the north and about ten inland from the river. Sergio Aguera lived there before moving to Texas to work for the Butlers. His parents are very old.'

'Ramos would surely have headed for

home after he ran from the Wayfarer. If he made it, the community will close ranks to keep him hidden from men coming after him with guns. We'll be met with stony glances, and silence.'

'Oh yes. Perhaps even open antagonism and threats.'

'Smoke ahead,' Guthrie said abruptly. 'Just appeared above those trees. Wasn't there a few minutes ago.'

Velvet located it, and her face was troubled. 'It could be peasants who've rolled out of their blankets, thrown wood on the fire to cook breakfast. But somehow I don't think so. There are no villages in the vicinity, so they'd be a long way from home. There's no reason for honest, hard-working men to be here by the river.'

'Miles away from home then, but not peasants,' Cage said, gazing ahead. 'One possibility is that they're lighting a fire to heat a running iron and brand calves.'

Guthrie nodded, his face tight. 'I'd go for that and, if so, then we could be in for trouble unless we stay well clear. Branding this close to the river suggests rustlers drove a small herd across in darkness. They're in a hurry to place their mark on stolen cattle.'

'I accept that it could be rustlers,' Velvet said, 'but why stop to do the branding now, this close to Texas? Why do it at all, if it comes to that? Once across the river, Mexicans are safe in their own country.'

'Before we crossed the river,' Cage said quietly, 'I thought I heard the crackle of distant gunfire. Anybody else hear that?'

'I heard something that could have been shooting,' Guthrie said. 'I thought it was the Texas side of the river, which is why I just suggested rustlers in one hell of a hurry.'

While talking they'd been moving their horses across open ground at a steady walk, still heading for the trees. The smoke from the fire was a white pencil line against the clear blue sky. Cage could smell it, the resiny wood, and with it came the mouth-watering aroma of frying meat. A meal was being cooked, but now Cage could hear a sound, a regular scraping followed by thuds he couldn't identify.

'What's going on?'

Guthrie was frowning, staring ahead.

'I don't know. But that was a horse whinnying. They've caught our scent.'

'Then there's no turning back,' Cage said.

'I can see movement through those trees,' Velvet said. 'Tethered horses, several men — Mexicans, by the look of their hats — watching something or someone, doing, hell, I — '

The shot ripped through the trees, came close enough to Velvet to cut her off in mid-sentence. It was followed by a fierce volley. Gunfire crackled. Muzzle flashes winked along the length of the stand of trees. At least three gunmen were firing. The air was hot with flying lead.

Cage threw himself from the saddle. He landed heavily on ground like solid rock. The jolt sent a stab of pain through his damaged cheekbones and nose. Eyes watering, he flashed a glance to his right and opened his mouth to yell at Velvet to go to ground. It would have been wasted breath. The slim woman had slid from the saddle as sinuously as a garter snake and was already belly down in the coarse grass. On the way she'd slipped the carbine from its boot. It was rammed into her shoulder. She was drawing a bead on the trees, her finger curled around the trigger.

Guthrie, the bank manager, was slower to react. Still up in the saddle, bathed in bright sunlight, he was staring towards the trees as if dumbfounded.

A sitting target.

Cage yelled, 'Are you planning an early grave?'

Guthrie appeared not to hear Cage's warning shout, but a bullet thudding into the saddle horn uncomfortably close to his groin brought him back to reality with a jerk. He yelped, toppled from the saddle, and Cage heard him grunt with pain from the still tender bullet wound in his shoulder.

He'd fallen without any thought for a weapon. Cage had also left the saddle thinking only of saving his skin, and again he felt admiration for Velvet Goodwine and her quick thinking. But at least he had kept a tight grip on the reins as he fell. Now, taking advantage of a lull in the firing, he pulled the frightened roan to him and was able to reach up for the Winchester. He grasped the butt, slid the weapon out of the boot and released the reins. The roan whirled, head thrown back, teeth shining, then galloped back towards the river taking the other horses with it.

Cage set his jaw, racked a bullet into the Winchester's chamber and fired five rapid shots at the trees.

'You're wasting ammunition,' Velvet called. 'Hold your fire, let them figure out what to do next.'

'Yes, ma'am,' Cage said, and he

grinned across at her and cautiously raised his body to peer through the long grass.

'How many are we up against?' Guthrie called. His voice was unsteady. He was lying prone, as flat as a grown man could be without sinking into the earth.

'Those three trigger-happy *hombres* in the trees, a couple more by the fire — I think,' Velvet said. 'Trouble is, I don't see any cattle.'

'So we could be wrong, and there's more to this than trigger-happy rustlers,' Cage said, then dropped flat again as the crack of a rifle was followed by the frighteningly close whisper of a bullet, another that was low enough to snick a blade of grass close to his head.

The shots were followed by an uneasy silence.

Into it, Velvet said softly, 'If not rustlers, then why were we met with bullets as soon as we were spotted?'

'Bandits,' Cage said. 'Been up to no good, on the lookout for *Rurales*.'

'No.' Velvet shook her head. 'They've got eyes, they know we're *Americanos*, and anyway bandits need something to steal, somebody to rob — and around here there's nothing — '

She broke off, swore and dropped her head into the grass as another volley of shots hummed through the air.

In a voice that was too high-pitched Guthrie said, 'I'm getting out of here,' and he began to wriggle backwards.

'Wait,' Cage snapped.

The bank manager stopped. His face was white, with an unhealthy greenish tinge.

'Before you do anything stupid,' Cage said, 'just listen.'

In the silence following the latest burst of gunfire, he had heard voices. Quiet at first, suddenly they became louder, more excited. Then there came to their ears the crash and crackle of brush. The gunmen, he thought. Abandoning the woods. There's a boss giving orders. They're being called back.

'They're leaving.'

That was Guthrie. Relief spilled from him. He laughed shrilly and pointed. A bunch of riders emerged from the trees on the far left and raced away from the river, bright sombreros flapping from neck cords.

'You see,' Velvet said. 'Do nothing and they get nervous. They've come back across the river, done something bad over there, broken the law, and this is still too close to Texas for their liking.'

'They think we're US lawmen,' Guthrie surmised.

'But they left one man behind,' Cage said, squinting into the distance. 'Now, what's that about?'

'One man we can handle,' Guthrie said, suddenly brave. He was up on his feet, looking towards the river bank where their three frightened horses had come together and were now grazing.

'Maybe,' Cage said, rising with care and dusting himself off, his eyes watchful. 'I've learned from painful experience that the best of traps are the simplest, the easiest to fall into.'

Velvet was already up, holding the carbine cradled in the crook of her arm with the familiarity of a woman born clutching the weapon.

'If there is a trap, sorting it out is up to you and me,' she said, looking meaningfully at Cage. 'We'll go and investigate. The bank manager can stroll across in the warm sunshine and wait by the horses for our signal.'

'I guess what she means,' Cage said tactfully, 'is if we're gunned down, you get the hell out of here, Guthrie, save your own skin and take news of what's happened to Frank Bellard.'

'Yes, I'll do that,' Guthrie said, and he released a breath in obvious relief. 'You two, take care.'

He walked off towards the horses. Velvet looked at Cage, and shrugged. Then she turned her attention to the woods, and began to walk in that direction.

'How do you read this?'

Cage grimaced. 'Damned if I know.'

'But the instant attack on our

approach means those men were up to no good, and this close to the river . . .'

She didn't finish. Like Cage, as they drew closer to the woods she could see that the Mexicans had indeed left a man behind. He was sitting on a fallen log in the shade, smoking a cigarette. That much was plain to Cage, but he sensed from Velvet's reaction that she was seeing much more.

'Well I'll be damned,' she said softly. 'You couldn't be expected to know, but the man they've left behind is Sergio Aguera.'

'Ramos's brother?'

'Yes. And you say that yesterday he was with Matt?'

'Rode away with him from the line cabin. My thinking was that they would cross into Mexico.'

'Looks like they did just that,' Velvet said, and this time when she looked at Cage there was compassion in her dark eyes. 'But if so, and that wild bunch had ridden off leaving Aguera there on his own, then where the hell is Matt?'

11

Sergio Aguera was a scrawny man dressed in the loose, off-white cotton garments of a peasant. His skin was the colour and texture of old leather. He could have been aged forty or seventy, but as Pepe Ramos's younger half-brother he had to be closer to thirty. The greasy black hair poking from beneath his frayed sombrero was ragged, his goatee looked as if it had been invaded by moths, but the hand that held the brown cigarette was lean and strong. More significantly, it showed no signs of the damage that would have been caused by hard work in the fields, which led Cage to speculate on Aguera's background, and just how much effort he had put into his employment with the Butlers.

Aguera watched Velvet's approach, his dark eyes alight, a smile curving his thin lips. As she drew near he rose from the log and clasped her to him in a warm embrace. Over her shoulder he looked at Cage without expression.

It had been clear to Cage ever since they rounded the trees that what this man had been doing — watched by the other Mexicans who had fled — was use his bare hands to carry what rocks and loose scrub he could find. With those materials he had attempted to cover a fresh mound of raw red earth. The mound was longer than it was wide, the shape an all too familiar sight in the West and leading to just the one terrible conclusion.

Cage took a deep breath, concentrating on the soft, comforting murmur of Velvet's voice.

'Sergio,' she was saying softly, 'do you recall Matt talking about a brother who left home many years ago?' She'd stepped back, one hand holding the carbine, the other remaining briefly on the Mexican's bony shoulder. Like Cage, she had seen the rocks. Like

Cage, she knew they could be serving but one purpose.

'Of course.' Aguera nodded. 'He spoke of him many times.'

'His name is Cage.' Again the nod from the lean Mexican. 'It was Cage who was there at the line cabin, with the lawman, Fitch. Fitch wanted to take Matt in to Bellard's jail, but Cage was there to help Matt, not to hurt him.'

'I understand, now. But now is too late.'

For a moment there was quiet. While Velvet and Aguera had been talking, Cage had drifted across to the pile of rocks. He was remembering the earlier rattle of gunfire, half heard, misinterpreted, imagining what lay beneath those stones. There was no feeling of grief. He had been away from home too long, Matt Butler had been a child when Cage rode out and in any case there were no ties of blood. But this was the third death in a family that had adopted Cage and looked after him without reservation as if he were their second son, and so, now more than ever, somebody must be made to pay.

Instead of grief, there was smouldering anger.

Still facing the heaped rocks, he looked sideways at Aguera.

'Tell me what happened,' he said.

The Mexican spread his hands.

'It is a simple story,' he said, and he swept off his sombrero, and held it in front of him with his hands on its broad brim. 'When we rode very fast from the line cabin it was with the intention of crossing at once into my country. But Matt, he wanted to see again what was left of his home. We rode to those blackened ruins. Matt spent a few minutes paying his respects.'

Sadness swept over Aguera's face. His eyes flicked towards Cage, from the man to the pile of stones.

'Matt knew, didn't he?' Velvet said.

'That he was seeing his home, his country, for the last time?' Aguera shrugged. 'That is possible, though for the wrong reason: Matt was convinced that he would die bravely and with honour, hunting down the men who had murdered his parents.'

'But it never came to that, did it, so what went wrong?' Cage said. He moved away from the stones and sat down at the end of the log the Mexican had been using. He was aware of Velvet retaining her hold on the carbine as if there was still an undercurrent of danger, and he placed his own Winchester across his knees.

'We crossed *el río* without the precaution of looking over our shoulders,' Aguera said simply. 'That was a big mistake. The men who burned down Matt's house had again crossed into America. It is my opinion that they were covering a lot of ground, looking at other ranches. For instance, there is the ranch owned by the Flanagans, stocked with herds of fine cattle.'

'Too good to miss,' Cage said drily. 'They were planning for the future.'

'There were six or eight of them, in high spirits,' Aguera continued, 'and we crossed unaware that they were behind us, had seen us and would watch us from across the water. They stayed out of sight for the afternoon, saw us make camp for the night. Then they waited under the stars, drinking, laughing, discussing what they would do.' His smile did not reach his eyes. 'That is not certain, it is what I imagine. But what I know for sure is that this morning, before we awoke, they came after us.'

'Picked their moment,' Velvet said, looking away, talking as she completed the story to her satisfaction. 'A difficult crossing, the river's deep here. But I'd guess that by the time you woke up, crawled out of your blankets, they were up the bank and at you. They shot Matt like a rabid dog, let you live but forced you to cover his body while they ate breakfast.'

Aguera nodded.

'You know what this means, don't you?' Velvet said to Cage.

'Many things,' Cage said. 'Which one

are you singling out?'

'You'll have to ask John Lawrence for confirmation, but I'd say Matt's death leaves you owner of the Butler spread. The house may have gone, but there's still the land.'

Cage sensed Aguera's swift look. He hesitated, trying to digest what Velvet had said; how, if he permitted it to do so, the inheritance could change his life. He felt dazed. Struggling to get back on track, to stay in the present not dream about the future, he addressed Aguera.

'Do you know those men?'

'Some are from my village. From San Luis.'

'And they're the same men who for the past couple of years have been stealing Al Butler's cattle, taking away any chance he had of making a living?'

Again Aguera nodded.

'Jesus Christ,' Cage said, up off the log, his voice tight with anger. 'And what about Pepe Ramos, your half-brother? Was he one of those rustlers preying on my family before he made his big mistake? You know he beat a man severely, then served time in jail?'

'Pepe was never a part of the rustling,' Aguera said. 'He is a man of honour, with principles, and so when he heard the name of his younger brother — and by extension the name of his family — being insulted by white Americans he had no choice but to — '

'The fight was in the Wayfarer,' Velvet cut in. 'I didn't think it important, Cage, but Pepe began waving a knife and it was Frank Bellard who sent him to prison.'

'If doing what he did makes him an honourable man,' Cage said, 'what about you, Aguera? Men from your village, stealing from your employer, yet you did nothing to put a stop to rustling that ended in tragedy. If you had . . . ' He shook his head helplessly. 'If you'd stopped that rustling,' he said, 'there's every chance that it would have ended there, and the Butlers would not have finished up as charred bodies in the blackened ruins of their home.'

'Come on, Cage, what could Sergio do, then or now?' Velvet said. 'He stayed with Al and May to the very end, and when they'd gone he remained loyal to Matt. That put him in danger. What surprises me is that he's still alive.'

'Yeah, me too. All right, maybe there was nothing he could do to halt the rustling, but that's all changed.' Cage was furious, pacing angrily. 'The men who did this are from his village. Aguera will take us there. He'll identify the men, and we'll — '

'Talk to them?' Velvet had one eyebrow raised, her lips pursed. 'Or do you propose to walk into a peaceful pueblo and start shooting?'

'Whatever's necessary.'

'I don't like it. And it's not going to be as easy as you make it sound. You'll be up against it, we'll be up against it. Those men will have loyal friends. We'll certainly be outnumbered — and that's assuming we manage to make it into the pueblo.'

'You're wasting your time, I'm not arguing.'

She stood, absently rubbing the carbine's barrel, clearly frustrated by his obstinacy. Then she shook her head.

'No, and neither am I,' she said. 'I'll go with you, make sure you don't do anything foolish. Right now I'll go and find Guthrie, tell him all's well and we're ready to ride.'

'He won't be of much use in a fight.'

'Three has to be better than two, and at the very least he brings the threat of another gun.'

Brush crackled as she jogged her way through the thin timber. Aguera had been listening in silence. His cigarette had burnt down. He flicked it into the grass, stepped on it, then walked slowly to where his horse was tethered in the shade of the trees. Cage noticed for the first time that the Mexican had a pistol at his hip, a rifle in a saddle boot.

Very soon, he thought, Ramos's half-brother would have a difficult decision to make: he would be asked to point the finger at guilty men. It was very likely that their response to any accusations would be violent. In those circumstances, would Sergio Aguera stand alongside Matt's half-brother, a stranger, when the opponents were not white men but his compatriots, his countrymen?

His thinking was interrupted when Velvet Goodwine returned much too quickly.

'He's gone,' she said. 'Milt Guthrie's left our two horses standing and lit out. The odds are back to what they were: if we press on it's just the two of us against Christ knows how many Mexicans who have killed more than once and will have no compunction about doing so again.'

12

It would have been easy to castigate Milton Guthrie for his cowardice, yet Cage knew that most sensible men would have wholeheartedly praised the banker's actions. From the lush banks of the mighty Rio Grande, Cage found himself riding ever deeper into Mexico. Ahead of him, their horses kicking up choking clouds of dust, were Velvet Goodwine and Sergio Aguera — and, despite the young woman's assertions, Cage was not yet inclined to trust the wiry Mexican.

That being the case, Guthrie's hasty departure seemed entirely reasonable. Accompanied by a young woman he could trust, and a Mexican whose allegiances had not yet been determined, Cage was venturing into a foreign country following the trail of a band of rustlers who had murdered

Matt Butler in cold blood. The killers were less than an hour ahead. They would certainly expect to be followed by the men they had tried to gun down with their rifles, but would be unlikely to have the taste or the stomach for a bloody face-to-face shoot-out. Cage's guess was that they'd lie in ambush. Between the river and their pueblo they would know of numerous twisting arroyos from the rocky ridges of which they could wipe out their pursuers with a deadly hail of hot lead.

It was a dun-coloured landscape. Searing overhead sunlight flattened shadows, but the terrain the trail cut through rose and fell, at times steeply. On several occasions already the horses had clattered through narrow arroyos, hoofs echoing from the walls, Cage and Velvet Goodwine lifting their eyes nervously to the rims. Out in the open, ever watchful, through the shimmering heat-haze Cage frequently caught sight of stands of parched trees closing in on the trail. They too could hide gunmen and horses. And although it was bordering on madness to believe that the temperature had rocketed when they crossed the river's cool waters, Cage couldn't rid himself of that impression. The sun beat down from a sky that was damn near white, and he was constantly using his bandanna to mop his face. That discomfort distracted him, broke his concentration, and increased his vulnerability.

Not a pleasant thought. It wasn't an exaggeration to say that failure to keep his wits about him would put his and the young woman's lives in danger.

Though Aguera had called Pepe Ramos an honourable man, Cage couldn't rid himself of the idea that the 'breed was now a member of the outlaw band they were trailing; had, perhaps, been the one to pull the trigger and fire the shot that ended Matt Butler's life. The only light to come from that thought was that Cage had spent a year in a cell with the 'breed, knew the man reasonably well, and might expect him to treat Cage and his companion with favour should it come to a bloody confrontation.

Yet even that idea was flawed. Using the heavy knife he wore at his belt, Ramos had brutally murdered Guthrie's wife, for no apparent reason — which seemed to prove that Cage knew the 'breed not at all.

* * *

They had been riding for an hour when Velvet dropped back and brought her pony prancing alongside Cage's roan.

'Don't know if you've noticed, but the village is not too far ahead. It's hazy, lots of dust, but you can see the white adobes sprawled like sheep on the hillside.

'I don't mind admitting I wasn't expecting to get this far.'

'Mm. You've been very quiet.'

'Ideas come and go,' Cage said, 'and few of them make sense. We can't imagine what lies ahead, so my biggest worry is that I've dragged you into a crazy venture that could cost you your life.'

'I seem to recall standing in my rooms at the Wayfarer and volunteering to ride with you.'

'You had good reason. That was when I was setting out to look for Matt. That reason was taken away by a well-aimed bullet.'

'Certainly was, and I can see that it puts what we're doing into question. Guthrie turned tail, so I don't have to stand between him and Ramos, so that's another reason wiped out. That leaves the rustlers who killed Al and May; and Matt, of course, which means they wiped out the only family you ever knew. Leaving you the proud owner of a Texas ranch. But that's not the point, is it? Going after the killers is highly commendable, shows great courage, but it's also foolhardy. Two of us, against a whole village?'

'Well put, but it's already been said and it still doesn't solve anything.' Cage grinned crookedly across at her. 'Tell the truth, I'm doing this by the seat of my pants, and if that sounds too much of a risk for you — '

'Oh, cut it out, Cage, you're constantly offering me a way out and that's disrespectful, and hurtful. Anyway, you'd be lost without my clear thinking. And, in case you haven't noticed, it's already way too late for doubts — '

'It's never — '

She cut him off again with a sweeping arm gesture, and when he looked where she indicated he saw that the men they had been following had not needed the convenience of an arroyo for their deadly work. Instead they had split up, kept a distance ahead and out wide on the flanks. There they had blended with their native landscape, becoming as one with the trees, the shrubs, the sun-baked terrain. Now, presumably because Cage and his companions were drawing close to their village, they had broken cover. Ragged, unshaven horsemen, multi-coloured sombreros like fragmented rainbows in the sunlight, were moving in from both sides with the sun glinting on their levelled rifles.

'Damn me, will you look at Aguera, riding over to meet those fellers?' Cage said softly.

'Oh, my goodness,' Velvet breathed. She watched for a few moments, then edged her horse even closer to Cage, reached out to touch his hand. 'He doesn't look like a simple ranch hand, does he, nor even a friend of those men. What he looks like is — '

'A *honcho*,' Cage said bitterly. 'He's not discussing the weather with those *hombres*, he's issuing orders. That throws into doubt everything he said at the river, his whole relationship with the Butlers.'

'Doesn't say much for my judgement of character.'

'No, but it does explain a lot. You say I inherit the spread. But it's not beyond the bounds of possibility that, with Matt *and* me out of the way, that crafty Mexican comes up with papers proving he's the new owner. Hell, they could even be genuine. If Al made a will, with the loyal employee Aguera last in line . . . '

'And it was me got Aguera the job with the Butlers,' Velvet said. 'God, I feel physically sick — ' Then she broke off and thumped Cage's arm hard in warning as Aguera swung his horse and cantered towards them.

'You switched sides, Aguera?' Cage said, going straight for the jugular.

'There was no need. For a true Mexican there is only ever one side.'

Aguera grinned, and suddenly Cage saw a glimmer of hope when he heard the slur to the man's speech, the eyes that were wet and bloodshot; the unsteady hands that suggested a bottle of mescal tucked away in a saddle-bag, sly drinks taken all the way across country from the Rio Grande.

'Those years working at the Butlers', you were sneaking word to your countrymen, right? Got your foot in the door, rode down to the town from time to time and spoke to your pals over drinks in the Wayfarer. Told them the best time to cross the river and steal Al's cattle. And all the time enjoying a roof over your head, three square meals, a few dollars jingling in your pocket.'

'And now there is the possibility of an improvement in even that exceptional situation,' Aguera said.

'Don't hold your hopes up. That place won't fall into your lap. Al wouldn't leave the spread to one of his workers.'

Aguera shrugged. 'It is true that there are no papers, no documents.'

'And no surviving blood relatives, but if you go talk to John Lawrence I'm pretty sure he'll tell you the Butler spread now belongs to me.'

'But you cannot be found,' Aguera said reasonably. 'In Nathan's Ford they know only that you rode into Mexico with the woman from the Wayfarer. After a certain time, when nothing is heard from you, rumours will circulate. *Cage and the woman were set upon by bandits. They have been murdered for their horses and their weapons.'* He grinned again. 'In Mexico, it is very easy for a person to disappear without trace.'

'Is that what's about to happen?'

Aguera shrugged. 'If a decision had been made you would have died by the river. There would be three graves there, not just the one.'

'Which means you're not sure. We thought you were the *honcho*, but you're not, are you? You're small time, a rat of no consequence, there's somebody much bigger than you — '

'But in this situation I have always the choice, to make the decision here and now would be sensible.'

'Then you'd better make your mind up, and fast,' Cage said, 'before our friend Guthrie returns with the kind of men who treat rogue Mexicans like the vermin they are.'

'Oh no.' Aguera grinned. 'Guthrie lit out, deserted you. Isn't that what the lovely Velvet said by the river?'

'That was for your ears, but not necessarily the truth.'

'My ears believed it then, and they believe it now,' Aguera said. 'No one will come to save you. And with all this wasteful talk at an end — '

He broke off as an explosion of action left him with his mouth hanging open, his bloodshot eyes wide with shock.

Still close to Cage, Velvet Goodwine freed one foot from a stirrup. She lashed a fierce kick at the roan's rump, hauled on the reins to spin her own horse in a tight turn on the hard earth, then spurred away from the Mexicans in a cloud of dust.

Stung by the kick, the roan squealed, lifted both forefeet from the ground then used its powerful back legs to drive it forward in a mighty bound. Its startled lunge almost unseated Cage, throwing him back in the saddle. He made a frantic grab for the saddle-horn as the big horse broke into a gallop that saw it thundering into the bunched

Mexicans, scattering men and horses like startled, squawking hens.

The direction the roan took left Cage and Velvet fleeing in opposite directions. At that moment, Cage didn't consider the consequences. Velvet had taken the initiative. She was clear and running free, he was through the Mexicans and they had yet to react. Knowing that every second they remained frozen saw him put another few yards of clear ground between him and the gunmen, Cage flattened himself along the roan's neck and gave it its head.

It was a big horse. The ride from the river had been a leisurely canter in the sun that had used up none of its great strength. Now, feeling the reins slack and its rider urging it on with whispered words and the lightest of strokes from steel spurs, it opened its legs and stretched out in a run that saw the ground flying away beneath its flashing hoofs.

It was several breathless seconds before the first shots rang out. When they came, the fierce detonations from the Mexicans' rifles had already been reduced by distance to a faint, harmless crackling. And with the eager roan in full flow and the wind whipping his hair, Cage was cautiously elated. Velvet Goodwine's bold move had left the Mexicans stunned.

Cage, his mind racing, had the gunmen down as simple peasants, with little grasp of tactics. Aguera was proving himself to be from the same stock, for a sound tactician would instantly have split the men into two groups and sent one group hard on the heels of each of the fleeing riders. Furthermore, confident that Cage and Goodwine were unaware of his duplicity, Aguera had been drinking since early morning. Velvet Goodwine's bolt for freedom — a bold move which had carried Cage with her — would have left Aguera staring helplessly at receding clouds of dust while struggling to think clearly through a fog of hard liquor.

Looking to him for orders, but getting no response, his men had opened fire. But their shots were flying wild. Their aim was frustrated by the nervous horses they straddled, their own panic, the clouds of dust and the glorious speed of the roan's eager running. And within a very short while the roan's ground-eating strides would have carried Cage well beyond the maximum range of their rifles.

But those moments before he could consider himself truly safe added urgency to Cage's own decision-making.

Velvet Goodwine was riding a small pony. It had endurance aplenty and was a fleet runner, but the Mexicans would still have Velvet in their sights. They would be trying to gun her down, firing old rifles with damaged or non-existent sights, and watching their bullets fly high and wide. Even simple peasants would quickly realize that they were wasting lead. And when Aguera finally got control of his addled senses, he would launch them into a hot pursuit of the fugitives.

When that happened, Cage wanted to be with Velvet. But Velvet had taken off in an easterly direction. That way lay the Rio Grande. Cage's flight was taking him north-west, towards the hillside pueblo and more danger.

With a swift glance over his shoulder that told him he'd left the Mexicans almost a quarter of a mile behind him, Cage pulled the lathered roan back to a less frantic pace and began a looping manoeuvre that would carry him in a wide half-circle and see him heading back towards the river. As he commenced that altered course, he was given reason to smile. The roan's eager flight had kicked up a dust storm. There was a slight breeze blowing. That breeze was carrying the hanging dust from north to south, which meant that it now lay between Cage and the Mexicans. A smokescreen provided by nature was, for a while, hiding his intentions.

It was short lived. The screen was being dispersed by the very breeze that had sent it drifting between Cage and his pursuers. With the circle he had begun only half completed, the dust had thinned enough for the Mexicans to be in sight again, now away to Cage's left. They had stopped their futile firing, and were in a huddle. Aguera must have snapped out of his drunken stupor and found his voice. The men were listening to his words — which were accompanied by much arm waving and the flourishing of a sombrero — and when Aguera finished speaking there was an explosion of action.

From the huddle of riders, three broke away and set their horses at a dead run across the open grassland. If Cage continued on his present course, they would quickly cut him off. Suddenly, the fact that they were simple peasants had lost its reassurance. The odds were in their favour. They were heavily armed, and if these were the same men who had savagely put Al and

May Butler's home to the torch with the old couple inside, they would show Cage no mercy.

Even as those bitter thoughts crossed his mind, fresh orders barked by Aguera were carried faintly on the breeze. Flicking a glance to his left, Cage saw three more mounted men detach themselves from the group and begin racing towards the south. If something wasn't done to stop them, they would quickly overtake Velvet Goodwine.

Reacting instantly, taking the only course open to him, Cage swung the roan hard towards the south-east and kicked it into a fast gallop. At once the situation changed. Cage was now on a line that would take him *behind* the three Mexicans attempting to cut him off — and already they were looking anxiously in his direction and taking note of the roan's speed and altered course.

Cage was bearing down on them fast. There was a flurry of dust as the Mexicans reacted by hurriedly dragging their mounts to a slithering halt. Horses snorted. Hoofs flashed, bared teeth gleamed white. The Mexicans began yelling, hauling on the reins, desperately pulling their excited horses around to face the threat from Cage. But panic saw them turning in on each other. Slick, lathered hide caught the sunlight as squealing horses collided, twisted, reared. Flailing hoofs raked human flesh, drawing forth howls of pain. Men struck out angrily with their fists, used their feet to try to escape the tangle — and then Cage was on them, and his six-gun was spitting flame.

He streaked past without slackening the roan's pace. The way the three Mexican horses were entangled made their riders sitting targets. Cage's first bullet knocked one man clean out of the saddle, his second hit another in the soft underbelly and doubled him over, his third drilled a black third eye in a sweating forehead and that man too went backwards out of the saddle to lie crumpled amid flashing hoofs.

Then, as Cage urged the big roan to even greater speed and raced to intercept the Mexicans running down Velvet Goodwine, three spaced shots rang out. At once, the three Mexicans gave up their pursuit. With wary glances towards Cage, they turned their horses and made their way slowly back towards Aguera and the remaining men.

For some damn reason they had been ordered to abandon the chase, and all Cage could do was breathe a silent prayer of thanks. He and Velvet had been granted precious time. What they had to do now was use it to their advantage.

13

Cage didn't catch Velvet Goodwine until she had streaked across the wide expanse of sun-baked open grassland and reached the banks of the Rio Grande. She was dismounting from her weary pony some way to the north of the mound of stones, scrub and raw red earth marking the spot where Sergio Aguera had buried Matt Butler. Nevertheless, wildlife had quickly detected the presence of a dead body. Flies buzzed in the hot air. At Cage's approach a black vulture flapped lazily away from grey-green cottonwoods. By comparison to those sights and sounds, the river was a gurgling murmur of relative cleanliness and purity in the background, a wide silver ribbon glittering through the trees.

Velvet had found the ruins of an adobe dwelling — little more than the remains of three bare walls. In the front wall the windows and doorway were gaping black holes. The roof was nothing more than the tangled, leafy branches of a big cottonwood that had grown across the derelict house. Ironically, what was left of the building was almost opposite the burnt-out Butler spread which was set a little way back from the bank on the American side of the mighty river.

Cage followed Velvet's example, dismounting, but going one step further by stripping the rig from his horse and dumping the jingling equipment up against the crumbling adobe walls. As he slapped the roan's rump, sending it off into the longer grass after Velvet's pony, she was watching him speculatively.

'I'm surprised you stripped the rig. You feel safe? You reckon we've seen the last of those fellows?'

Cage eased his stiff shoulders, shook his head.

'The horse'll be all the better for a

spell without the saddle, but, no, we've not seen the last of them. Leastwise, not if I have anything to do with it. You know my reasons for crossing the river: I was hunting unknown killers, but since Aguera showed his true colours that task's been made easier. I have a name. That name will lead me to others. Or perhaps that's not necessary. If Aguera turns out to be the man responsible for the rustling, the horrible death suffered by those old folks, then making him pay for those crimes will be enough. Either way, I go on. We've suffered a setback, but nothing has changed other than for the better.'

'I wouldn't say that. Señor Aguera underestimated you. He won't do that again.'

'As I recall, it was you who made his hair stand on end, not me.'

She grinned. 'That was drink slowing him down. Without that advantage, I wouldn't have got away with it. Sergio's seen me at work in the Wayfarer. He knows I'm impetuous, a firebrand, not inclined to pull punches.'

'All right, so he was sneaking sly drinks on the ride in because he figured I was a pushover, he and his men could take me as easy as snapping fingers. But you changed all that with your sucker punch, so why now has he backed off?'

She bent to her saddle-bag, extracted a water bottle and threw it to Cage.

'*Mañana*.'

Bottle uncorked, half-raised to his mouth, Cage paused. '*Mañana*? What's that supposed to mean?'

'It's a philosophy. Haven't you heard of it? Mexicans look lazy, never appear to be in a hurry; it's as if they have all the time in the world. Soon after my shock tactics had hit him fast and hard, Aguera's eyes were opened even wider when he saw you kill three of his men and set off after the others. As there was a good chance you'd have downed them, too, he fired those shots to pull them back. The way he figures it, what's the rush? We were riding away, so we were no longer a threat. Either we cross the river and that's the end of it, they can't touch us, or we hole up somewhere on the Mexican side for the night' — she waved a hand, indicating the adobe, the lush grassy banks — 'and they can come after us nice and easy and take us at their leisure.'

Cage took a drink. The water was surprisingly cool. Sparkling droplets dripped from his chin, dampening his shirt. He tossed the bottle to Velvet, looked at her shrewdly.

'But not necessarily tomorrow?'

'Oh no. That word shouldn't be taken too literally.' She smiled wryly. '*Mañana* might mean the next day, or some indeterminate time in the future. It could also mean in a couple of hours, because I don't expect Aguera to wait long.'

'And your best guess is?'

'Dusk. No, I think perhaps a little earlier.'

Cage thought for a moment, then nodded his agreement. 'The sun sets in the west.' He hooked a thumb over his shoulder. 'They'll be coming from that direction, riding in with guns blazing and the sun a blinding light shining directly into our eyes.'

'If you've no taste for it, we could cross the river as soon as the horses are rested,' Velvet said softly. 'Say to hell with the lot of them.'

'And go where, do what?' said Cage. 'I have no home, no family. For that loss, someone must be made to pay, and pay dear.'

'Yes, of course,' Velvet said. 'I fully understand your anger, and you know my reason for riding with you. I have a fondness for Pepe Ramos. He was in prison for a reason he considers honourable, and I do not for one minute believe he murdered that banker's wife.'

'Well, as we're both set on staying in this Godforsaken land, for whatever reason,' Cage said, 'I think we should look to our weapons, mumble a few of our favourite prayers, then get some rest.'

He looked thoughtfully across at her as he picked up his bedroll and unlaced the ties.

'If it makes you feel any better, I've just this minute recalled some details, something I heard said. If my memory's not making a fool of me, it was nigh on impossible for Ramos to be responsible for Guthrie's wife's murder.'

* * *

Sunset came and went.

Cage and Velvet Goodwine had rested for several hours. They did little more than doze, but lay comfortably in the shade, expunging all thought from restless minds and letting the cool air wafting in from the river begin to lift the salt sweat from their skin.

Velvet had risen with a yawn as soon as Cage rolled off his folded blankets. They'd drunk more of the cool water and made a crude meal of the supplies they'd brought with them — tough jerky and hard biscuits. After that, a brief discussion had been all that was required to settle on tactics. Hell, Cage had said, they'll attack, we'll defend as best we can, what else is there to work out?

We could, Velvet said somewhat belatedly, have taken the fight to the enemy. Then she'd rolled her eyes. Cage had merely shrugged, while wondering uneasily if they'd done their thinking too late.

And so, as the golden orb of the sinking sun touched the rim of distant western hills, they had taken up their positions inside the ruined dwelling, each to one of the window openings. Alongside Velvet lay her Spencer carbine, and she had twirled her belt around her slender waist so that the butt of her Beaumont Adams revolver was more easily reached by her right hand.

Cage, equally outfitted, but with Colt and Winchester, thought that in the fading evening light Miss Velvet Goodwine looked as pretty as a picture

— albeit one with latent menace. The shirt was blood-red, her skin as pale as alabaster in contrast to the dark of her tied-back hair and flat-crowned hat.

She caught him watching her. Her dark eyes shone, and in the gloom Cage couldn't tell if he'd detected the faintest of flushes, or if it was an illusion created by the shadows.

Didn't matter, anyway. The Mexicans chose that moment to attack.

And instead of coming in from the west with the sun at their backs, they came out of the darkness from two directions, riding north and south towards the adobe along the banks of the Rio Grande.

On those sides of the ruined dwelling, there were no windows and near as dammit no walls. Not only were Cage and Velvet cruelly exposed, the first volley of shots from the Mexicans riding upstream sent Cage's roan kicking and squealing down the river bank in its death throes.

'That's one hell of a start,' Cage

shouted. Then he dropped to one knee to take advantage of what cover the almost non-existent side walls provided, and opened fire with his six-gun.

He chose those attackers coming in from the south. They were riding in hard and fast, crashing through and around the cottonwoods. Their guns were blazing, vivid bursts of lurid flame poking holes in the dusk. But they were firing from the saddle, the jouncing of their ponies ruining their aim. Hot lead from their pistols peppered the cracked adobe, skittered through the high branches or whined off rocks, leaving Cage untouched.

Behind him, Velvet Goodwine was unhurried, firing carefully spaced shots at the men coming down river from the north. Both she and Cage had sensed instinctively that, despite the lack of cover and the overwhelming odds, they held a slight advantage. Facing fierce volleys of wild shots fired by peasants unskilled in the use of their weapons, they were shooting from a braced position on level ground, picking their targets. Cage had downed three of the attackers. He knew Velvet would be having the same success.

But the wild onrush of mounted men was an unstoppable force. They came thundering on from two directions, guns blazing, the pounding hoofs drawing ever closer. The shooting was incessant, a barrage chipping stone and wood splinters, plucking at clothing. Cage and Velvet were forced to grovel, hugging the raw earth. The sheer volume of lead expended meant that sooner or later one or both of them would take a bullet. If that didn't happen . . . well, Cage fully expected the Mexicans to simply ride them down, spurring their lathered ponies in over the remains of the walls and chopping at Cage and Velvet's bloody flesh with the barrels of rifles and six-guns.

They didn't do that.

Instead, inexplicably, the gunfire was cut off. The sudden silence was eerie.

The onrush slowed. Then, as it drew close to the ruined building, each group veered away and the half-dozen men left in the saddle cantered rapidly away to come together again and take up a position some 200 yards away to the west.

'Where we expected 'em to be at the outset,' Cage commented, rising cautiously against the front wall and dusting himself off. 'Did you spot Aguera?'

'Yes, he was there. I think I heard him shout.'

'What about you? You OK?'

'Never better,' Velvet said. 'But they made a hash of it, didn't they? There are bodies out there, their companions, dead, soaked in blood. And the next time they attack, when they launch an assault from that direction we've got the cover we had planned.'

'That's if we stay.'

He sensed her quick look. 'D'you have a better idea?'

'A wiser one. Yes, we'll now be covered by that front wall when they attack. But we're still outnumbered — and they might not do that anyway. If you think about it, there's that *mañana* business you were on about.'

'Yes, indeed, there is, isn't there,' she said thoughtfully. 'We chose this position, but did we think it through? It's easily defended, but it's also a trap. If they encircle us on the landward side they can sit and smoke their cigarillos or cheroots, knock back gallons of mescal or whatever the hell they drink, and watch us starve.'

'But what they cannot do,' Cage said, 'is keep us away from the river.'

'Exactly what I was thinking. Can you swim?'

'No.'

'Hell. Your horse is dead, my poor pony can't carry two — '

'So let's thank the Lord you had the foresight to leave it saddled. Bareback this would be impossible, but as it is you can ride across and I'll cling to a stirrup and try to keep my head above water.'

'They'll see we're trying to escape, do their best to stop us. A pony can swim only so fast.'

'The pony will swim, the river's current will help by carrying us downstream.'

'But never faster than men on horseback, riding along the river bank. They'll be taking their time, pouring bullets at our defenceless backs, and we'll be out in the open. It's a big risk, Cage.'

'We rode hard back to the river to get out of a tight situation. The way I see it, we've ended up worse off. Staying put means certain death; making a try at crossing the river gives us a slim chance.'

She cast an angry glance across the hundred yards or so separating them from the Mexicans. They were gathered at the edge of a stand of trees, silhouetted against the last of the sun's ruddy light. Cigarettes glowed in the gathering gloom. Even at that distance, she could pick out Sergio Aguera.

She bit her lip, shivered, then nodded decisively.

'Those fellers, they're different, somehow. I thought I knew Aguera, but I can't figure the way he thinks, the way any of them think — and not knowing what their next move's going to be scares me half to death. So, yes Cage, we'll run like bats out of hell to my pony, and I'll take it straight down the bank into the water and start swimming for it — but we do it now, and we do it fast before my courage leaks out of my boots.'

Cage chuckled. 'I heard a certain lady describe herself as a firebrand, not one to pull punches, so that kind of talk fools nobody,' he said, and the glance he cast at her was full of admiration. 'I'll carry my Winchester, leave everything else behind. You said make it fast, Velvet, so on the count of three . . . '

The south wall, nothing more than a low ridge of crumbling adobe, was shaded by trees, the night already growing dark enough to make their break for freedom go unnoticed from any distance. They slipped out of the ruined adobe without haste, moving slowly to avoid detection, and walked steadily out of the trees. Then, once out in the open and exposed, they threw caution to the winds and sprinted down the river-bank to where the pony was nervously grazing alongside the dead roan.

Almost at once they heard distant cries of alarm, followed by chaos into which Aguera barked a command. Then Velvet had thrown herself on to the pony's back and Cage was struggling to keep up as she spurred it down the bank. At the last moment she kicked it hard with her heels. The pony responded gallantly, leaping forward to plunge into the waters of the Rio Grande and send up a great gout of glittering spray.

Recklessly, Cage flung himself after them. He hit the water flat. The panic of a non-swimmer caused his outstretched hand to slip off the slick leather of her boot. Then his clawed fingers caught and locked on the stirrup. Pain knifed through his shoulder as his arm was almost wrenched from its socket. He opened his mouth in agony, swallowed what felt like half the river, and went under, choking. He thrashed and kicked wildly, tried to clutch the Winchester as it slipped out of his other hand and was lost. Then, hanging on to the stirrup with the strength of a man frightened of dying, he broke surface, gasping like a fish — and heard the crackle of the first shots and the strange splat and hiss of bullets hitting water close to his face.

Velvet's weight was forcing the little pony under the water. She was lying flat along its back, her fingers locked in the long mane. The pony was kicking hard, fighting, lunging, but kept sinking beneath the surface. Its neck was straining upward, veins and sinews like taut rope, its teeth bared as it struggled to breathe through cold water lapping at its flared nostrils.

Cage's weight dragging on the stirrup was also unbalancing the animal, holding it back and pulling it down. Though the pony was swimming hard, snorting wetly, its eyes were rolling and they were making little progress. As Cage had predicted, the current was taking them downstream. But the drift was slow, and they were still dangerously close to the Mexican bank.

As the pony weakened, it turned with the current so that it was facing downstream. That left Cage exposed to the half dozen mounted gunmen who had thundered past the adobe, ridden down the bank and were keeping pace with the floundering horse. Cries rang out, then bellows of jeering laughter as Cage stared wildly towards the bank, clinging desperately to the stirrup.

The shooting had stopped, but one man with long greasy hair restrained by a filthy headband urged a ragged pony to the fore and lifted a big pistol. He had a patch over one eye. With his good eye he squinted, and took aim at Velvet

Goodwine. That was his big mistake. Flattened along the horse's neck, Velvet managed to draw her six-gun and snap a fast shot at the Mexican. He cried out hoarsely. Then the gun flew from his hand and he toppled sideways off his horse to splash into the shallows.

At once cries of rage rent the night air. Pistols were raised, aimed. Muzzle flashes flared red in the gloom as lead rained down on the couple in the river. Cage clenched his teeth as something hit his left hand a mighty blow. The bolt of agony was like a knife blade being thrust under his fingernails and all the way up his forearm. Strength leaked from his muscles. His grip on the stirrup loosened, his lifeless fingers opened, let go. As the water began to suck him down he desperately flung his right arm across his body, reaching with his good hand for the stirrup. At the same time Velvet saw his plight. Her pistol splashed into the water. Keeping a tight grip on the pony's mane, she leaned out and down as far as she could. Her arm reached out to Cage. Their fingertips brushed.

Then the river swept him away.

He'd heard that drowning was an easy way to die. The last thing he wanted was to put that theory to the test, but he was fighting a losing battle. Weighed down by his clothes and filled boots, he went under, arms and legs thrashing wildly, his eyes wide open. Clamping his lips shut, forcing himself not to breathe yet already starved of oxygen, through clear water aerated with a froth of bubbles he saw the pony's legs working. With Cage's weight gone, it was able to swim freely. It had again turned towards the far bank. Its renewed strength was taking it away from Cage.

Then Cage's eyes blurred. Flapping feebly, he broke surface once, tried to time a gulped intake of breath with the fraction of a second that his head was clear of the water. Instead, a wave kicked up by the pony's thrashing hind legs hit him in the face. Expecting air, he greedily sucked in pure water. Immediately his lungs felt as if they were on fire. Agony forced his mouth wide. The instinct to survive made his body try again to find air, but he was under, and sinking. Again he sucked in water, and now he could feel his eyes bulging from their sockets.

Lungs burning, weakness slowing already feeble movements, he thought he could feel his toes dragging across the gravel of the riverbed. Then as if in a dream he floated, drifted. Pain became a thing of the past as he was overtaken and overpowered by a comforting blackness that robbed him of all feeling, all thought — all life.

14

Cage came to his senses with a tremendous weight pressing on his back. He was aware of his clothes being soaking wet, of lying face down in rough shingle, of aching from head to foot. His eyes opened slowly. His vision was blurred. He blinked, squeezed his eyes a couple of times, shook his head — and thought it would split. Then, as the weight came down again and again, he opened his mouth and his throat and stomach spasmed as he vomited an acrid mixture of bile and river water. He retched again, spat, then groaned like a dying steer.

'Jesus Christ,' he said hoarsely, 'will you quit doing that and let me get my face out of this mess?'

There was a rich chuckle. The weight was removed. A hand touched his shoulder.

And a voice he recognized said, 'Miracles occur, *si*? This has been one of them. He will live — you think?'

* * *

Half an hour later Cage was sitting with his back against a tree. His right hand had been bandaged with strips of a brilliant red cloth that looked familiar. The bullet had torn straight through the web between thumb and finger. No bones or tendons had been damaged.

In front of him the grassy bank sloped gently down to the river. Behind, perhaps a quarter mile away, could be seen the blackened ruins of the Butlers' ranch house.

A small fire was glowing in a circle of rocks. In the heat of west Texas it was not required to warm chilled bodies, but Velvet Goodwine had decided that as most of what Cage had eaten at the adobe had finished up on the shingle at the river's edge, he needed sustenance. Hot food, this time, not cold jerky.

Washed down with strong black coffee.

She was sitting cross-legged in the shade. Pepe Ramos was also cross-legged, out in the hot sun but shaded by his tattered red and yellow sombrero. Inevitably, he was toying with his knife. The blade flashed, matching the brilliance of his toothy grin.

'About now,' Cage said, 'is the time to begin telling how I escaped from the jaws of death.'

'The first thing Pepe did,' Velvet said quietly, 'was make just about the best throw with a rope I've ever seen. It dropped over your arm as you waved your last goodbye.' She grinned. 'Then, when my pony staggered up the bank, carrying me to safety, he used his rifle to even better effect. Those men were certainly going to come across after us. Dear Pepe made them change their minds in a hurry.'

Cage looked at Ramos with suspicion. 'How did you happen to be here, just when you were needed?'

'For now, I live here,' Ramos said,

grinning. 'I was here when you came with your brother, I watched you arrive, I watched you leave.' He jerked a thumb over his shoulder. 'There are outbuildings, used for stores, untouched by the flames . . . it is there I found the rope.'

'So where are they now, those men who damn near succeeded in killing us?'

'Doesn't matter,' Velvet said. 'Our Mexican adventure is over — isn't it?'

She looked quizzically at Cage, and her eyes widened as he shook his head emphatically.

'But we have no weapons. You have no horse. Your hand needs professional treatment.'

'Then we go to town and fix all that. But when we get there, before acquiring horses, weapons or supplies, I go to Frank Bellard. I'm going to make it clear to him that Pepe Ramos could not have killed Guthrie's wife.' He glanced across at Ramos, ducked his head. 'After what you've done for me, my friend, that's the very least I can do.'

Ramos grinned. 'You think?'

Cage rolled his eyes.

'What *I* think,' Velvet said, 'is we go to town, and once we've all calmed down we'll take it step by step and see where we end up.'

'*Paso a paso*,' Ramos agreed. 'It is an idea of some brilliance.' He nodded, slipped the big knife into its sheath and sprang lithely to his feet.

* * *

Velvet's pony struggled on the way in to Nathan's Ford. The distance was quite short, the slow canter across lush Texas pasture not arduous, but the little horse had worn itself almost to a standstill. The desperate flight from the Mexicans, across open land in searing temperatures, had been at a frantic pace. Then had come a brief period of rest followed almost at once by the valiant struggle to carry two people across the Rio Grande. The bullet had almost been the death of Cage, but it had saved the pony, and Velvet.

From the river bank to Nathan's Ford, Cage rode double with Ramos. Though the 'breed was keen to hear how Cage could possibly clear his name, Cage kept that information to himself, feigning sleep as he clung to the 'breed. It was, he felt, best to keep quiet until he was face to face with Marshal Frank Bellard. Bellard could then telegraph the news to Dave Eyke, and from that point it would be up to the Drystone marshal to hunt down the real killer.

It was close to midnight when they rode in, the sky bright with stars, the town deserted, oil lamps casting pools of warm light on to empty plankwalks. There was a light glowing deep inside Elliott's livery barn — an old man having trouble sleeping, Cage figured — and, surprisingly, across the street the door to Marshal Frank Bellard's office was open and two men could be seen inside the lamp-lit room.

'Bellard and your friend, John Lawrence,' Velvet said quietly, drawing the tired pony level. 'What the hell are they doing, up this late?'

'Chewing the fat,' Cage said. 'It's something they do regularly, but I'm sure you know that.'

'Nevertheless,' Velvet said, frowning. Then she shrugged. 'You go ahead, Cage. I'll take my pony across to Vern Elliott, face his fury when he sees her condition, and leave her to his expert ministrations.'

Ramos said nothing. Cage sensed the tension in the man: the last time the 'breed had been confronted by Marshal Bellard he had run for it and thrown himself bodily through the saloon's window.

They left Velvet and crossed the street. With the horse tied at the hitch rail and both men up on the plankwalk, Cage gripped Ramos's arm.

'Stay cool,' he said, feeling the man's rigid muscles. 'I'll go in first. Trust me: a couple of minutes from now you'll be a saint with a shiny halo.'

Nevertheless, that was not how Frank Bellard saw it.

The town marshal was behind his desk, coffee cup in hand. He looked up as Cage stepped inside, saw at once who was behind him and coffee slopped all over the desk as he came out of his chair in a rush with his six-gun already out and raised.

'Careful, Frank,' John Lawrence said warningly. He was in a chair near Bellard's desk. He was holding a smouldering cigar, and had the imperturbable demeanour of the professional lawyer.

'No need for care,' Cage said, 'but common sense would come in handy. That, and a willingness to listen.'

'I'll listen when that man's locked up,' Bellard said tightly. He was trying to get past Cage. Cage was blocking him resolutely.

'No crime has been committed — '

'Dammit, that feller cut a woman's throat.'

'No.' Cage shook his head. He had his good right hand flat on Bellard's chest. The marshal batted it away angrily, glowered and flushed an angry red when it was replaced.

'Just listen, then think back to what you heard,' Cage said, gazing levelly at the marshal; and he waited, watched Bellard take a ragged breath, step back. 'When I was there, in John Lawrence's office,' Cage went on, 'you came in for your regular talk and told John that Guthrie was in town, and how his wife had died. I took no notice at the time, but the murder scene as you described it was wrong. Or, if it was right, then Ramos is no killer.'

'It was right,' Bellard gritted. 'I got it straight from Dave Eyke, and he's not a man to make mistakes. But how does what he said let Ramos off the hook?'

'I'm not denying we were in the house — me, and Ramos — and we had a bank robbery all planned. But when we got there, Guthrie and his wife were in bed. We were in the place no more than five minutes. When I left the house with Guthrie, when Ramos left the house no more than a couple of minutes later — *that woman was still in bed.*'

'She was dressed,' Bellard said. 'Lying sprawled across the breakfast table, her face in her own blood.'

'Then by the time her throat was cut she had risen from her bed, got dressed, fixed breakfast and was sitting eating . . . and by that time the brief spell exchanging shots in town with Dave Eyke was over, and me and Ramos were on the run.'

'Her body,' Bellard said expressionlessly, 'was discovered by her husband.'

Cage nodded. 'And Ramos here will confirm that while we were in the bedroom, the woman said something about Guthrie wanting her dead, that he'd like that . . . '

'I'm quite sure you're right,' John Lawrence said, 'but if the banker killed his wife, or paid someone to do the job, it makes little difference now. Milton

Guthrie's dead, Cage. He died trying to come back across the river. 'Stead of riding down to the ford, he crossed higher up, in deep water. It was a gamble — and he lost. His horse came trotting into town. A while later Guthrie's body was discovered a mile downstream. Looked like his horse threw him, and that foolish man had never learned to swim.'

15

It was two in the morning. In the Wayfarer just one table was occupied. Over it, a single oil lamp sputtered, as if running out of fuel. Or perhaps the fuel was contaminated with water.

Velvet Goodwine, hair loose, trousers and red blouse — part of which had been used to bandage Cage's hand — replaced by a comfortable, colourful robe, raised an eyebrow as she caught Cage looking at her with an appreciative smile. Across from her, dark-suited Alan Spence was flaunting his paunch and looped gold watch chain and drinking some of her most expensive whiskey. Light flared as he struck a match and leaned to one side to apply the flame to John Lawrence's cigar.

At a nearby table, in deep shadow, the match's flame was reflected from the cold steel of an ugly blade. Pepe

Ramos was holding his knife upright; the blade's point poked into the rough wood of the table; the tip of his forefinger rested on the end of the hilt and with his middle finger and thumb he was rotating the weapon slowly, one way then the other.

'You see,' John Lawrence said, his eyes tired, 'although you have indeed inherited Al Butler's estate, you are still left with nothing. The house was burnt to the ground. No stock grazed on the pastures. And because the place was mortgaged to the hilt, those valuable acres — which is all that's left — have for some time belonged to the bank.'

'Perhaps Velvet will give you a job,' Alan Spence said, and at once he chuckled to soften the derisive quality of his words. 'One thing about a place like this, selling hard liquor to thirsty cowboys, there's never a shortage of buyers.'

'If I restock the spread,' Cage said, eyes distant, 'with land that good I can bring it back into profit. If the stock costs me nothing — and it would have to — then so much the better.'

'There is some trouble which I can see at once,' said Ramos out of the shadows. 'The stock about which you speak, the stock that will cost you nothing because, of course, you would steal it back from the rustlers, is scattered all over Mexico.'

'And,' Velvet said, 'venturing back across the river for any reason at all is surely one hell of a risk.'

'Doesn't concern you,' Cage said mildly. 'Alan Spence has had enough of running a saloon, you're needed here.'

'Not at all,' Spence said. 'I've never in my life had so much fun.'

'And besides, you know that it does concern me,' Velvet said, 'because I consider myself partly to blame for the mess you find yourself in, for the losses you have suffered. If I hadn't got Aguera that job with the Butlers, none of it would have happened.'

'The blame is widespread, I think,'

Ramos said. 'It was clear for some time that Aguera was arranging the theft of cattle, yet none of you could see it; many blind eyes were turned. And then, when he began aiming higher and burned down the house — '

'What — are you saying it was Aguera who did that?'

Ramos smiled sadly at the fury in Cage's voice. 'That, yes, and he will continue doing the Devil's work, if permitted. I went to prison for defending the honour of a man who has none. It is surely up to us to stop him — you think?'

'I think,' Cage said, nodding, his jaw set. 'It's been my aim ever since his evil was uncovered: to go after Aguera, and the cutthroats who worked alongside him.'

'The intention is admirable, achieving all of it is an impossibility, and in any case unnecessary,' Ramos said. 'Yes, it was Aguera who put the word out, but each time it was answered by men from different pueblos. The men who crossed the river at his call are gone for good, as widely scattered as the cattle they stole.' He grinned at Cage, waggled the knife. 'Though he will be protected by loyal *compañeros* who will put up a fight, they are as nothing. It is just the one man we go after: Aguera. It is surely true — you think? — that if we cut off the head, the body will be incapable of causing any more trouble?'

'If you mean get rid of the boss then the others will fade away, I couldn't have put it better,' Velvet said. 'And if we're going to do that, no time should be wasted and there's outfitting to do. My pony's out of it, Cage, and your roan's dead, so we need horses, guns, and supplies.'

Cage scraped back his chair. 'We do, but you don't. You rode into Mexico with me and Guthrie to make sure Ramos came to no harm. This time, Guthrie's dead, and Ramos has been cleared. He rides with me, but after the close shave we had out there I can't allow you to risk your life yet again.'

'We're also desperate for sleep,' Velvet said, ignoring Cage's words and pushing on blithely. 'I suggest the three of us meet at dawn, over at Vern Elliott's barn. He'll have horses there we can hire or buy outright. A little way down the street, Ike's general store's got the rest — guns, shells, food.'

'Dammit,' Cage said, 'you're not listening, are you?'

Velvet smiled sweetly as she pushed back from the table.

'Actually, you're the one not paying attention. I'm going with you — alongside with your approval, or tagging on behind, either way suits me. Oh, and just to keep you on your toes, to give you a gold-plated reason for coming through this with your hide all in one piece, I've been doing some serious thinking.'

'Which means?'

'That when this is all over, I'll have a pleasant surprise for you. For you, and for Alan.'

And with an enigmatic smile and a swirl of the robe, she winked at Spence's puzzled look and wafted away into the Wayfarer's back room.

16

The plan was a sensible one, as far as it went: the three of them would cross the river at dawn, ride steadily to the pueblo where Aguera's family home was located, find the man and . . .

And what?

That was the trouble. The plan went so far, and no further — and, against the Lord knew how many armed men, so far wasn't quite far enough to ensure success. In his bones Cage knew that they could be riding into a heap of trouble. That night, in his room at the Alhambra, he was an uneasy man who slept fitfully and awoke with nothing settled in his mind.

Indeed, at times he had found himself questioning his motivation; questioning why he was putting other people's lives at risk to bring in one man. The stolen cattle were scattered far and wide. Nothing he could do would bring back Al, May and Matt Butler. And, hell, his own record wasn't whiter than white, so who was he to pass judgement?

Feeling like death, Cage tramped downstairs, red-eyed. In the grey pre-dawn light, he, Ramos and Velvet Goodwine ate breakfast served by an unshaven and disgruntled cook in the Alhambra Hotel's dining room. Breakfast finished, plates pushed away, Cage and Velvet sat back. They were finishing their coffee. Cage could sense Velvet watching him. He was gazing fixedly out at the empty street, contemplating in silence the dangers he knew lay ahead.

Ramos was also draining his coffee cup, and smoking a thin cheroot. Against the black leaf of the tobacco, his teeth gleamed white. His sombrero hung on the back of his chair, a splash of colour in a sombre room. His knife was in the sheath fashioned from laced hide. His dark eyes were knowing as he looked at Cage.

'It is very early,' he said, and he gestured expressively. 'This hostler, Elliott, in the livery barn, he is old. He will awake sluggishly — perhaps we will need to slap him a couple of times.' He grinned. 'Then, I am sure that he will take his time with the horses we select, perhaps haggle over the price. And the other, *la tienda*, the general store. It will open much later. When we arrive there — on our new, fresh mounts — it will perhaps be very busy. Women and children, very noisy, very talkative, selecting clothes, candy, passing the time of day with the owner — '

'What's all this leading up to, Pepe?' Velvet said.

'Such circumstances decree that we will not cross the river at dawn. And if we are careful, if we play our cards right, we will not reach the Pueblo San Luis before nightfall.' He raised an eyebrow. 'Which, *en mi opinión*, is an accidental happening, but an improvement to the plan of last night — you think?'

'What I think,' Cage said, feeling a weight lift from his shoulders, 'is that you have hit the nail on the head. Going in in broad daylight was a crazy idea. We make sure we sneak into the village well after dark; better still, after midnight. Everyone's asleep, even the dogs. We make our way to Aguera's house — Ramos, you know where Aguera lives?'

'For God's sake, Cage,' Velvet said, 'they're brothers, Aguera's home is Pepe's home.'

Abashed, Cage nodded. 'All the better. And the layout of the house?'

'A couple of rooms,' Ramos cut in, and winked at Velvet. 'Aguera, like all of the villagers, is a *campesino*, a peasant, not *un ranchero caballero*.'

'Right.' Cage nodded. 'And there's one other point I want to make clear.' He looked at Velvet, then at Ramos. 'We find Aguera, and we bring him in alive. Understand?'

'Our understanding is one thing,' Ramos said. 'It will be difficult, I think, to make Aguera see things our way.'

'It's surprising what men will agree to,' Velvet said, 'when they're staring into the muzzle of a gun.'

She'd left the table while talking, and now paused and looked at the two men.

'I'm going over to the Wayfarer. Alan Spence will be coming in soon, and I want to go over the books with him, see if he's made a profit in those hours I was absent, or robbed me blind.' She dismissed that thought with a smile. 'I might as well be there as hanging around town. And you two . . . ?'

'Hang on here for a while,' Cage said. 'Drink some more coffee, go a bit deeper into how two men can steal into a sleeping village and leave, with a prisoner, without raising the alarm.'

'Tricky,' Velvet agreed, 'but I'm sure we'll manage. OK, I'm off. You get what you need, I'll spend an hour with Spence in the saloon, cross the street and talk to Vern Elliott about a fresh horse then trot down to the general store to sort out a weapon.'

'If you see to the supplies while you're there, that would be helpful,' Cage said.

'Lord above, how long are we going to be away, Cage? If we have a good meal before leaving I can't see us needing much more than fresh water and biscuits.' She mulled over that idea, then nodded. 'Right, so with all that done we'll all come together . . . where, and when?'

'The livery barn, again,' Cage said, 'because the horses will be left there for the day. And I'd say an hour after sunset.'

She nodded again, looked at him hard as if about to comment, then lifted a hand and turned away. The door clicked behind her as she left the hotel.

Ramos was holding his cheroot close to his lips, watching the smoke rise but looking through it at Cage.

'It did not escape my notice,' he said, 'that although Velvet will be riding alongside us when we leave town and cross the river, you mentioned only two men stealing in and out of Pueblo San Luis.'

'Two men going in, three coming out — that's what I meant.'

'But no mention of a woman.'

Cage nodded. 'You're very quick.'

Ramos grinned. 'What is it they say? The quick and the dead?'

'Exactly. I'm sure I must have been thinking along those lines,' Cage said, 'when something told me that changing the plan was the right thing to do.'

17

It was an hour before sunset when Cage and Ramos crossed into Mexico.

They splashed across the Rio Grande using the stony ford a little way to the north that gave the town its name, the spray kicked up by their horses carried on the slight breeze as a sparkling nebula of stars drifting weightlessly to fall and dapple the flat surface of the river. Jingling and crunching through shallow water and across wet gravel, the two horses sounded like the vanguard of an army on the move. Cage was unperturbed. The Mexican killer they were hunting could be miles away, asleep under blankets in a distant pueblo, or he could be watching their approach from a lookout point some way back from the river. If the latter, then silence would be of no significance; Cage and Ramos could be as quiet as field-mice, and still not escape Sergio Aguera's eagle eye.

They had left town with consummate ease. Always fearful that Velvet Goodwine would spot them and realize their intentions, they had strolled down the plankwalk with an air of supreme nonchalance and, at the last second, slipped into the shadows of Vern Elliott's livery barn. There they had made a final check of their guns and equipment, mounted their horses and left the barn by the rear doors. The narrow, rutted back road ran parallel to the town's main street. Through the occasional side alley cutting between buildings they caught glimpses of the town, oil lamps already being lit. When they walked their horses out of the road at the edge of town they were almost upon the sandy slope down to the river and a good hundred yards to the west of the Wayfarer saloon.

Once across the river, Cage led the way to a line of cottonwoods on the bank a quarter mile to the north. There, the two men dismounted. They had left town earlier than intended. The stillness all around suggested that they had crossed undetected, but now they needed full dark as cover before pushing deeper into Mexico.

'It is my belief,' Ramos said, his black eyes glinting in the flare of a match, 'that Aguera has the cunning of a fox.'

'Proved it by his actions over the years,' Cage said, sitting loose in the saddle, hands folded on the horn. 'Is there a point you're making?'

'I am not sure. My half-brother, he is in a situation best solved by keeping his head down until he is a very old man. He has no hope of owning the Butler spread. In America he is wanted for cattle rustling, and for murder. So, why show his face?'

'My guess is he won't. That's why we're going after him.'

'And if that is precisely what he is hoping for?'

Cage sighed, swept off his Stetson and slapped at a cloud of mosquitoes.

He dragged a canteen from his saddle-bag, drank deeply.

'Ramos,' he said, 'if you've got something to say, for God's sake spit it out.'

The 'breed's cigar-end glowed. He shrugged his shoulders.

'We are . . . how you say, committed? We could turn back — but it was your family he slaughtered and your face tells me letting him go free is not an option. So, in the darkness as we ride, we must keep our eyes and ears open. For something that is not right. For any . . . trickery. You understand?'

'Yes and no,' Cage said, packing away the canteen and replacing his hat. 'Your meaning's clear, but the way I see it, Aguera's dug himself into a hole and there's no way out. One of us is right, and I have a silver dollar that says it's me.'

They waited another half hour, then moved their horses out of the cottonwoods and set off across the open plain. There was no need for more talk. Cage was retracing the path taken with Velvet Goodwine and Milt Guthrie; he had rented a fresh horse from Elliott, and was armed with a new six-gun and Winchester repeating rifle. Ramos was on home ground, riding his own tough pony which could find its way blindfolded, carrying the familiar weapons that had served him well in the years before his time in jail.

As the sun's red afterglow faded, the landscape ahead and around them was bleached of colour by the light of the rising moon. Coarse grass became a drab grey-green. Stands of trees were thin charcoal smudges against the luminous skies, and mostly following the line of the Rio Grande.

They were riding at an angle away from the river, the horses cutting across the ragged terrain on a line that was the shortest way to Pueblo San Luis — the hillside village Cage had glimpsed briefly with Velvet Goodwine. Ramos was now pulling away from Cage. His pony was frisky, tossing its head, kicking its heels. Cage was aware of the 'breed, laughing softly as he gave the pony its head, drawing further away from him. The gap between the two men was quickly widening, but for several vital minutes Cage found himself distracted. His eyes were constantly drawn towards the river they were leaving. The moon was painting its flat surface silver. For some reason, that metallic sheen was putting Cage on edge — and he couldn't understand why.

Then his eyes moved north along the river bank, and he felt a stab of pain as he recognized the dark outline of the trees that hid the mound of earth and rocks beneath which Matt Butler had been laid to rest. Cage knew now what was disturbing him — and that unease surged towards the onset of panic as beyond the grave he saw the pale outlines of the ruined adobe. Suddenly he was assailed by a tumble of vivid images, sights and sounds that had him clenching his teeth. Foreboding swept over him like a chill black cloud as he recalled his arrival there with Velvet, the brief but explosive gun battle that had reached no satisfactory conclusion, and the burning agony tearing at his lungs as he sank beneath those silvery waters and into deep unconsciousness.

Cage's fears of impending disaster proved to be justified. As he shook his head in an effort to dispel the terrible feeling of gloom, he was shocked to see a lance of red flame spurt from the black square that marked one of the distant adobe's windows. It was followed almost instantly by the flat crack of the rifle.

Fifty yards ahead of Cage, like a bundle of old clothing, Ramos tumbled silently from the saddle to lie still on the ground.

Again the rifle cracked viciously from the adobe. This time the 'breed's pony was the target. When Ramos tumbled from the saddle, the startled animal had slowed to a trot, head held high, ears flattened. Now, as silently as Ramos had died, the pony's legs crumpled beneath it and it went down in a heap.

Cage raked his fresh horse hard with his spurs. It snorted a protest, then bounded forward. He drew alongside the downed horse, the inert man. Again the rifle cracked. He heard the whisper of shot cutting the air above his head. Cursing himself for being reckless and foolhardy, he slipped from the saddle and dropped down beside Ramos. He ripped off a glove, felt for the 'breed's throat, searched for a pulse — found none.

He could do nothing. The man was dead. Cage's priority now was staying alive. There was a burning desire within him to complete the task he had set himself: to bring to justice a wicked peasant who had insidiously taken a man's livelihood by theft, then destroyed the family with fire and bullets.

Cage was all too aware that the likelihood of his succeeding was becoming ever more remote.

For an instant, as he remounted and

set off across the plain, he wondered if his decision to leave Velvet Goodwine in Nathan's Ford had been wise. Then, as if to convince him of the wisdom of his actions, a picture of Ramos's crumpled body flashed into his mind. Instead of the 'breed's swarthy countenance he saw that of the young woman, her dark hair framing her lifeless face — and he knew he had been right.

The shots from the hidden rifle — perhaps more than one — were steady and persistent, the stabs of flame from the adobe like winking fireflies in the night. But the moon was still low in the sky, its light poor. Cage was now moving very fast, taking his horse across the line of fire. In good light it would have needed an exceptional marksman to hit him; if he took a bullet now it would be through sheer bad luck.

He had spotted a low rise some quarter-mile ahead. Tweaking the reins he urged the horse toward its solid safety, keeping his silhouette as low as he could to make that one lucky shot an impossibility. He reached the knoll in seconds, thundered around its northern flank. That put the high ground between him and the adobe. Relief was so great it was like a weakness. He sat up, slapped the horse's neck, felt the tension leak from his muscles. Then once more he slipped from the saddle. This time he plucked the Winchester rifle from its leather boot.

When Ramos was downed, Cage had ridden across the fire being directed from the adobe; to reach the knoll he had been forced to bear to the right. This had brought him around in a sweeping half-circle that meant he was now much closer to the river, and no more than a couple of hundred yards to the north of the building.

He jogged up close to the knoll's crest, then dropped to the grass and wriggled the rest of the way. There he swept his hat from his head and peered towards the ruins.

There was no movement. No sign of life.

The Mexicans had stopped firing as Cage reached the safety of the knoll. From the knoll's crest the faint white shape of the adobe and the dark overhanging cottonwood that was its matted roof looked exactly as it had when Cage first rode there with Velvet Goodwine: a building razed by time and the elements, the crumbling remains empty, deserted.

Cage smiled wryly.

That was an illusion. He couldn't understand why, but clearly Aguera had decided to stay at the adobe long after Cage and Velvet had made their escape across the river. Perhaps he had stayed behind to bury his dead, then remained to mourn. Again Cage smiled. If he had, the mourning had undoubtedly developed into a drunken wake as he and his men steadily emptied several jugs of mescal.

I'll bet, Cage thought, Aguera couldn't believe his good luck when, right out of a goddamn pale moon, I came riding into view with his half-brother. Probably figured there's a lot to be said for that *mañana* philosophy. That was his big mistake. Putting it in words Ramos himself would certainly have used, Cage thought grimly, *la verdad es que* I am here to prove him wrong.

With a feeling close to exultation, he worked the lever to insert a shell into the Winchester's breech. He planted the butt into his shoulder and fired four deliberate shots that sent bullets drilling into the ruined walls of the adobe. Waited. Listened to the fading echoes, the stunned silence. Fired four more shots, sent them rattling through the matted cottonwood.

Swiftly he slid backwards, rose to his feet and ran down the grassy knoll, at last hearing the sound of distant yells as the Mexicans reacted. From his saddle-bag he ripped open a box of shells and replenished the rifle's magazine. Then he slid the Winchester into its boot, mounted the horse and set off at a fast lick towards the river. He rode straight and true, knowing he was still hidden by the knoll, banking on the Mexicans anyway looking towards the knoll's crest for the source of the shooting.

The cool clean air coming off the river chilled the sweat on his face as he reached the bank and dismounted. The moon was now brighter. He was not too far upstream from the spot where he had almost drowned. Looking across the river and down a ways, he could see the slope up from the eastern bank, the blackened remains of the Butlers' house. He thought he saw movement, and guessed that foxes or coyotes were prowling about the deserted place without fear.

Then he took a deep breath. Returning his attention to his own troubles, he looked down the river's western bank.

He was no longer protected by the knoll. Some trees, faded cottonwoods, were all that stood between him and the adobe. If he attacked on horseback he would present a bulk difficult to hide and the trees would be of little use. If he made his way along the bank on foot, he could possibly move from tree to tree, shadow to shadow.

Then he remembered that the adobe's side walls were as good as gone. That was a small plus — leaving the Mexicans exposed — but also a big minus: the trees he was hoping to use for cover stopped short of the old dwelling; there was open ground to cross, and from the ruined building they couldn't fail to see his approach.

OK, Cage thought with a savage grin, let's make what they see not only memorable, but downright terrifying. If the trees are useless as cover, then there are no trees. The adobe has side walls that are a joke, and the big minus says there's nothing between you and the Mexicans — between you and Aguera. So turn that minus into a plus: go in fast, go in hard, make every man-jack of them so damned scared at what they see and hear they'll likely die of fright before you go leaping in with six-gun blazing. If they don't, if they're still alive — well, grown men who've soiled their britches will be in no condition to put up a fight.

Cage led the horse away into the grassy shadows under a stand of trees a little way inland, looped its reins around a low branch, secured the hitch. Again he checked his six-gun, spun the cylinder with its snub-nosed shells, tested the oiled action for smoothness. Then he drew the Winchester from its supple leather. With the tension again tightening his muscles he walked a little way across the lumpy ground, back towards the river bank so that he could see past the cottonwoods; those trees that in the next hectic minutes, for him, would cease to exist.

Time to go.

He forced himself to relax, to breathe through his mouth. Standing with his boots planted firm in the soft earth, he brought the Winchester tight into his shoulder and fired six shots. The muzzle spat flame, lighting the trees, driving back the shadows. The sharp detonations split the night. He directed each bullet into the black heart of that ruined building. Then he tossed the rifle on to the grass close to the horse and set off at a run.

Cage ran fast and hard, his boots ripping through the short grass. As he ran he yelled, he screamed; he damn near ripped his throat raw with the intensity of his howls. At the same time he flourished his six-gun high overhead, the bright steel flashing in the moonlight. He was an army officer, yelling exhortations, leading his men into action.

To the confusion of the Mexicans.

The Mexicans had seen Ramos die. They'd turned their fire on Cage, watched him ride for the knoll like the devil was snapping at his heels. Now he was boldly running at them, roaring his troops forward — though they had seen nobody. But they had been staring fixedly inland. Their backs had at all times been to the moonlit river. Had that been their mistake? Was there a possibility that from that other direction, coming in from those flat waters while the big American created his diversions . . . ?

Cage's raking strides gave them no time to think further. He tore past the drooping cottonwoods — touched the trunk of one, grinned because it was solid — and bore down on the adobe. As he screamed his rage, the ruined building seemed to be coming at him in a rush. Suddenly there was the open space, the naked red earth — then that low side wall. He went over it in a single bound, scraped a knee badly on jagged stone and fell and rolled as he gave one last banshee howl. Then, from the ground, he lunged for the higher front wall. He dropped into a corner away from the nearest window, into deep shadow, spun to face the room with his six-gun levelled.

It was empty.

His raw throat rasped a curse. The bullets from his rifle had been wasted. Aguera was not there. There were no men with sombreros in that cottonwood-shaded space, no men with dark unshaven faces, with evil eyes and levelled guns, no —

Then, even as that shadowy emptiness registered, it was filled.

A huge Mexican vaulted in over the low south wall. A second man, as thin as a rat, came in without haste over the northern wall — he had hidden and fallen in behind Cage's furious charge. Against the moonlight now flooding the river-banks Cage could see those dark shapes with guns levelled — guns that now wavered, hunted in vain.

As time seemed to stand still, Cage breathed his thanks to the overhanging cottonwood. Moments ago the Mexicans had been staring along the river-bank into his rifle's flaming muzzle, had leaped into the adobe out of moonlight that was growing ever brighter. Their night vision was destroyed, the darkest parts of that shaded room were in the angles formed by the front and side walls — and Cage was as one with the deepest of those shadows.

In the heavy silence that was like sudden deafness after Cage's demonic howls, he could hear the Mexicans breathing hard. For moments that seemed like eternity they were blind and helpless. That couldn't last. In a few short seconds they would regain their sight and see him hunkered in the corner —

Coolly, Cage shot the big man in the chest. He grunted, and in the gloom his shocked eyes gleamed white. The bullet knocked him backwards. He legs worked, jerkily, then stopped in time with his failing heart. Dead, the Mexican fell back across the jagged adobe wall with a sickening crack of snapping bone.

Cage's single shot was enough to give the second Mexican a clear target. Lightning fast, he snapped two shots at the muzzle flash. But Cage had downed the big Mexican, then instantly rolled to his right. He felt the second bullet clip his boot, returned fire and again threw himself to one side. And still he held the advantage. Though the dazzling flashes from the six-guns were now affecting both men, Cage was down low, the Mexican still outlined against bright moonlight.

As if reading Cage's thoughts the skinny shape dropped to the ground like a rope slipping from a wall, and was lost.

Cage's lips peeled back from his teeth in a snarl of frustration. He fired at the man's position, but dropped his aim to compensate. The bullet smacked impotently against stone; the rat-like Mexican had wriggled left. From his new position he fired again, again using Cage's muzzle flash. And this time Cage was slow to move. He hissed in agony as the bullet ripped a bloody gouge across the back of his left wrist.

Then, as he clenched his teeth and

threw back his head, a third Mexican slid silently through the window that was now above Cage. The man had the bulk and weight of a sack of grain. Thick legs straddled Cage. A meaty hand forced him down on to the cold earth. The Mexican's fingers clawed at Cage's shirt front. His other hand was raised high. In it there was a big knife.

The blade came down, flickering in the moonlight. Cage struck backhand with the six-gun. He felt the muzzle strike flesh, crunch the man's cheek-bone. The blade couldn't be stopped — but it was knocked to the side. It sliced across Cage's left shoulder like liquid fire, buried itself in hard-packed earth. The knife-fighter growled as he struggled to work it free.

Cage jerked his body, struggled to free himself — but in vain. Pinned down by the big Mexican's sweating bulk, he heard boots crackle on dry brushwood as the thin Mexican climbed out of the shadows and came storming into the fray.

Cage's left wrist was burning, his shoulder on fire. He twisted his head and saw the thin man silhouetted against moonlight, coming in fast with his six-gun raised to strike at Cage's head like a steel club. Desperately, Cage stiff-armed the muscular body pressing him down, somehow lifted the man off him with his bloody left arm. Then he threw his right hand across to the left, between their straining bodies. He fired once with the blood-slicked six-gun and hit the thin man in the groin, fired again as the Mexican folded in agony and saw him go down.

Then he pulled back the six-gun, pressed it to the big Mexican's chest and pulled the trigger.

The hammer dropped. There was a dull click. The firing pin had hit an empty shell.

Above him there was a grunt of triumph as the knife came free. The man reared up. Again there was a flash of steel as he lifted the knife, brought it down in a savage stab at Cage's throat.

Cage blocked it with his right forearm. The man's arm was jarred. The knife's point pierced Cage's shirt. He felt the hot sting of the cut. The empty six-gun fell from his hand. He held his forearm rigid, pushed the knife clear, grabbed the Mexican's wrist with his bloodied left hand. The man grinned. His teeth gleamed white under a drooping moustache. His hot breath stank of cigar. With insolent confidence he brought his left fist down like a hammer on Cage's left wrist. Cage's grip was broken. And as fast as a striking serpent the man lifted the knife high and brought it down.

Cage's desperate squirm almost tore him free. But the knife-strike was too fast. Cage took the blade in his left shoulder. The steel sliced into muscle. Pain was like molten metal flooding across his chest, pouring down his arm to his wounded hand. He roared, bucked fiercely, then twisted and bucked again, driving his hips high. To the Mexican it must have been like sitting astride an enraged Brahman bull. Despite his weight, he was thrown backwards. His hand was torn from the bloody knife. He slapped the ground as he fell sideways, struggling for balance.

Cage slipped from under him.

He rolled away — rolled across the warm dead body of the thin Mexican. As he did so he reached across to his shoulder and pulled the knife from his bloody flesh. It sucked free, the steel dragging open the raw lips of the wound. Cage was almost overcome by a wave of blackness and nausea. He gasped, struggled for air, then rolled again and somehow came to his knees, shaking his head to clear it.

He was given no time to recover.

The Mexican launched himself away from the front wall. He landed with both feet on his dead companion. Bone crunched as the dead man's ribs caved in. Then the big man's full weight hit Cage. He drove Cage back and down. His powerful arms wrapped around Cage's upper body in a deadly embrace. Cage's lower legs were doubled under him, his knee joints creaking, threatening to snap. His face was buried against the Mexican's chest. He twisted, opened his mouth to scream his pain to the skies, took a mouthful of sweaty cloth and gagged. Desperately, he kicked his legs straight. The relief was instant — but now he was flat on his back and fighting to draw air into lungs compressed by the weight that was like that of a full-grown steer.

The Mexican's big hands moved up to Cage's throat. His thumbs slipped under Cage's chin. He began to squeeze.

Cage was staring up at the dark canopy of branches, through them the stars, the moon. But he couldn't breathe. The night sky was becoming blurred, visible only through a red film. Almost lazily, almost without thought, he gripped the slippery hilt of the knife that was trapped between their struggling bodies. With his last remaining strength, he bucked his hips. The Mexican was concentrating on strangling Cage. For an instant he allowed his weight to be lifted. With his arm free to move, Cage twisted his wrist. Then the Mexican again bore down, growling angrily — and the roll of flesh under his ribs came down hard on the point of the vertical knife.

There was an instant when the stricken man quivered as if suffering a severe attack of the ague. Then, as if overcome by a second spasm, his hands loosened, his fingers uncurled, and with a soft sigh his whole body relaxed.

Somehow Cage struggled from under the leaden weight. Conscious of blood soaking his sleeve and the left side of his shirt, of a singing in his head that presaged the onset of unconsciousness, he moved clear then gritted his teeth and rolled the Mexican on to his back.

The man's mouth was open. His breathing was weakening, failing. His open black eyes were filming over.

'Aguera,' Cage said, but the word was

unclear, blocked in his clogged throat. He cleared it, spat, said, 'Aguera, where is he? Where is Sergio Aguera?'

And the dying man summoned a grin, a shake of the head. In his anger, Cage grasped the massive shoulders and shook him. The Mexican's head lolled. His lips pulled back from his teeth. The drooping moustache trembled as he struggled to speak, fluttered with breaths that would be his last.

'*La mujer*,' he said hoarsely, and his voice came whispering from the dark abyss. 'He has gone after *la mujer*, the woman . . . and now for you . . . it is much too late.'

And then he was dead.

18

He couldn't stand the scent of death.

With his hand covering his mouth Cage stumbled out of the ruined adobe and sank down on the grass where cool dew was settling. But the scent went with him. It was in his nostrils. He had left behind him three dead men, but the coppery smell that rose in hot waves from his own soaked shirt, the weakness that came over him in waves, told him that very soon there would be a fourth.

And that, he thought, would be of no help to Velvet Goodwine.

He placed a hand on the grass and looked back the way he had come, saw beyond the cottonwoods his horse grazing contentedly in the moonlight — and Cage knew he couldn't walk that far.

Did it matter? Within a few yards of

him the Mexicans' sturdy mounts stood quivering, clearly showing their own hatred of the stench of death. Cage could stagger across to one of them, cling to the horn, drag himself into the saddle — yet he knew that when it reached the gravel ford at Nathan's Ford, the horse he had chosen would be carrying a dead man.

And then, with sudden clarity, he knew that wallowing in a morass of self-pity was yet more time wasted. He was deliberately stalling. The movements he had seen across the river, in the shadows alongside the burnt-out Butler ranch house, had not been made by coyotes or foxes. Sergio Aguera had left his men at the adobe. They had orders to stop Cage and Ramos. A gun battle was inevitable. Aguera had reached Nathan's Ford, snatched Velvet at gunpoint, then taken her for a ride upriver.

At the Butler spread, they'd had ringside seats. Now Aguera was waiting with *la mujer*, the woman. But there was a river to cross — and Cage couldn't swim.

He took a deep breath. He made it to his feet, stood swaying. His own six-gun was empty, and lost. He stumbled through the black hole that was the doorway into the adobe, stripped the gunbelt from the skinny Mexican, found the man's six-gun at his feet and packed it with shells. Then he stumbled out over the side wall and walked unsteadily to the horses.

He chose one that looked as if it could swim, then laughed at his own foolishness and wondered if he was becoming delirious. Cage was soaked in blood. The horse began backing away. Cage grabbed for the reins, managed to hold on, made it into the saddle. The other horses wheeled away, cantered off into the moonlit distance.

Without hesitation, Cage took his mount down the sloping bank and they plunged into the waters of the Rio Grande.

* * *

In days to come, he preferred not to remember that ride. The horse could swim strongly, but Cage's weight kept pushing it below the surface so that the crossing was one long, desperate fight for life. Cage himself was in and out of the water — mostly in. Panic sent waves of pins and needles across his scalp. He held his face high, his mouth clamped shut, and opened it to breathe only when his lungs screamed in protest. He kept his eyes closed. The last thing he wanted to see was how far there was still to go.

Then suddenly there was change. There was a jerk beneath Cage as the horse found solid ground beneath its feet. It lunged, emerged from the river shedding water in sheets, went up the bank in a rush. Caught unawares, Cage didn't dismount. He fell off. He slid back over the horse's tail, hit the ground with both feet and slapped the horse hard on the rump. It kicked its heels and galloped up the slope. Cage stood swaying.

He dashed water from his eyes, fumbled at the holster searching for the Mexican's pistol. It was still there. As if in a dream, he drew the weapon, cocked it, and fired a single shot at the sky. Then he grinned happily. That solved one problem: the water hadn't put it out of action.

A low laugh greeted the shot. Cage blinked, looked up the slope and saw two figures step out of the shadows. Velvet Goodwine first. Behind her, Sergio Aguera. His arm was holding her hard against him. The muzzle of his six-gun was pressed to Velvet's ear.

'Jesus Christ Almighty, Cage!' Velvet said softly, and Cage saw her hand go to her mouth, her eyes widen with shock.

He didn't bother looking down, knew the sight he must present. He had entered the water with his shirt soaked in blood. The waters of the Rio Grande had done the rest. His clothes were heavy with water and, as the water soaked his clothing, the blood had spread. Walking towards them he was a horrific apparition, streaming blood, dripping blood, trailing blood. His eyes were blinking from a face that was a glistening red mask.

His appearance hit Aguera a shocking blow. A superstitious Mexican, his grip on Velvet slackened. The pistol eased away from her head. His mouth opened as he squinted in horror at Cage.

Velvet kicked backwards. Her hard heel raked Aguera's shin. He squealed in pain, started to bend. Velvet tore free, and ran. She ran towards Cage. She was thirty yards away, running down the slope — but she couldn't make it. Aguera saw the danger. His hostage had gone, but she was still between him and Cage. Ignoring the pain, Aguera lifted the six-gun, drew a bead on the running woman.

Cage had his six-gun up and cocked.

He yelled, 'God-dammit, get out of the way.'

He waved frantically at Velvet, urging her to one side, out of the line of fire. She saw him, swerved, slowed. And Aguera's pistol followed her.

As if in slow motion, Cage began squeezing the trigger. He knew that Aguera was doing the same, knew that their shots would ring out in unison; knew beyond any shadow of doubt that his bullet would hit the Mexican.

He knew, also, that he could not stop Aguera's bullet, could not save Velvet Goodwine.

Then, out of the night, a deep voice roared at the Mexican.

'Aguera, put down that gun and lift your hands!'

It was enough. Cage and Aguera fired as one, but Aguera was distracted, half turning as he fired. His bullet missed Velvet by a mile. Cage's took him in the throat, severed an artery. He went down choking, and died in a pool of his own blood.

* * *

'Ramos is dead,' Cage said.

Velvet nodded sadly. 'I guessed as much. Maybe . . . I don't know, could it be for the best?'

'The best is you being alive,' Cage said, 'and for that we have Alan Spence to thank.'

'I followed her, and got lucky,' Spence said, shrugging dismissively. The big man was still as Cage remembered him: dark suit, gold watch chain; and, unsurprisingly, the horse standing nearby was a thoroughbred. 'Saw her taken in town by that bastard, couldn't act fast enough, did the next best thing.'

'It was enough,' Cage said.

Velvet was bandaging his wounds as best she could. He needed urgent treatment by a doctor, but the bleeding had to be stopped.

'Oh, there's much more more,' Velvet said, her hands bloody. 'I've sold the Wayfarer to Alan. It's what we both wanted. I'm going to use some of the money to pay off the mortgage on this spread, the rest to restock — '

'But — '

She put a finger to his lips. 'We'll rebuild, have our own rooms but an office from where we can run the spread together: Cage and Velvet, the C slash V.' She grinned. 'No strings. And we'll see how it works out.'

Cage closed his eyes, felt sudden contentment.

'Maybe that should be the other way around, the V slash C,' he said. 'Knowing the way you handle business, I reckon we'll be bigger than the Flanagan place in no time at all.'

Other titles in the
Linford Western Library:

INCIDENT AT BUTLER'S STATION

Neil Hunter

For Cavalry Sergeant Ed Blaine, wounded by an Apache lance, the way station offered a chance to recover. All he wanted was a place to rest. But it was not to be . . . First he met up with the girl he had once been about to marry. Then he found himself under the guns of a bunch of outlaws waiting to free their brother from an incoming stage. Then, just when Blaine figured it couldn't get any worse, Butler's Station was hit by a band of warring Apaches . . .

NEBRASKA SHOOT-OUT

Corba Sunman

Jeff Arlen, a detective with the Butterworth Agency, is on the trail of Alec Frome, who has stolen $10,000 from the bank where he works. Riding into Sunset Ridge, Nebraska, he hopes to find Frome in the town where he'd once lived. But, soon after his arrival, he is drawn into a perilous local battle. Capturing Frome and retrieving the stolen money looks like child's play compared to what he now faces, which will only be resolved with plenty of hot lead.